CHANCE
MEETINGS

BOOKS BY WILLIAM SAROYAN

Novels

The Human Comedy
The Adventures of
  Wesley Jackson
The Twin Adventures
  *(The Adventures of
  William Saroyan Writing
  The Adventures of
  Wesley Jackson, and
  The Adventures of
  Wesley Jackson.)*
Tracy's Tiger
Rock Wagram
The Laughing Matter
Mama I Love You
Papa You're Crazy
Boys and Girls Together

Stories

Dear Baby
My Name Is Aram
Saroyan's Fables
Peace, It's Wonderful
The Trouble with Tigers
Love, Here Is My Heart
Little Children
Three Times Three
Inhale and Exhale
The Daring Young Man
  on the Flying Trapeze
The Saroyan Special
The Whole Voyald
The Saroyan Reader
I Used to Believe I Had
  Forever, Now I'm
  Not So Sure
Letters from 74 Rue Taitbout,
  or Don't Go But

If You Must Say Hello
to Everybody

Memoirs

The Bicycle Rider in
  Beverly Hills
Here Comes, There Goes
  You Know Who
Not Dying
After Thirty Years,
  the Daring Young Man
  on the Flying Trapeze
Days of Life and Death
  and Escape to the Moon
Places Where I've Done Time
Sons Come and Go,
  Mothers Hang In Forever

Plays

The Time of Your Life
My Heart's in the Highlands
Love's Old Sweet Song
The Beautiful People
Sweeney in the Trees
Across the Board on
  Tomorrow Morning
Razzle-Dazzle
Sam Ego's House
A Decent Birth,
  A Happy Funeral
Don't Go Away Mad
Get Away Old Man
Jim Dandy
  (Fat Man in a Famine)
The Cave Dwellers
The Dogs, or
  The Paris Comedy, and
  Two Other Plays

CHANCE MEETINGS

WILLIAM SAROYAN

W·W·NORTON & COMPANY·INC·

NEW YORK

Library of Congress Cataloging in Publication Data

Saroyan, William, 1908–
Chance meetings.

1. Saroyan, William, 1908–   —Friends and associ-
ates.   2.   Authors, American—20th century—Biography.
I.   Title.
PS3537.A826Z525 1978   818'.5'203 [B]   77–17505
ISBN 0–393–08809–X
1 2 3 4 5 6 7 8 9 0

This book is a greeting to my contemporaries living in Armenia and writing in Armenian: Hrant Matevosian, novelist; Vahagn Davitian, poet; Levon Muggerditchian, critic; Razmik Davoyan, poet; Sergo Khanzadian, novelist; Maro Markarian, poet; and Grikor Gourzadian, astrophysicist, painter-philosopher. And also a greeting to Armenak Saroyan, infant great-grandson of Armenak Saroyan of Bitlis, 1874–San Jose, 1911.

CHANCE
MEETINGS

THE THING about the people one meets on arrival, upon being born, is that they are the people they *are,* they are not the people any of us, had he indeed had a choice, might be likely to have chosen. These meetings are chance meetings.

Certainly everybody between the age of two years and twelve years has studied such people and questioned their right to be related in any way at all to himself. Himself, the very center of the world, the justification for all time gone, the supreme achievement of the expenditure of all effort, at last a flawless specimen. Both human and superhuman, if only the truth were known.

Are *these* people mine? This preposterous mad woman is *my* mother? This unbelievable loud-mouth man with the violent eyes is my father? How can such people be my people? There has got to be a very terrible mistake somewhere.

And of course there *is*.

There is this *same* terrible mistake back of every human being who is not yet thirteen or fourteen years old. And the mistake sometimes isn't corrected, or at any rate isn't *ignored*, even after the age of thirty. Now and then certain extraordinary people feel the pain of the mistake straight up to the event of death itself.

These astonished and hurt souls are the geniuses, but there are also geniuses who have deeply cherished their parents. And if they haven't both cherished and *loved* them, they have, at any rate, been so amused by them as to have never had any wish to have them out of the way.

And these *happy* geniuses, so to describe them, are frequently the best of the lot.

Mainly, though, geniuses are those who cannot be, or do not *want* to be, delivered from the feeling of being ridiculously involved in one colossal mistake.

It is the impulse, the compulsion, or the *wish*, to try to correct this horrible blunder that drives these people to work and has them bring forth all sorts of forms of improved variations of the original thing— that is, the whole mishmash, the whole universe, if you like, the whole solar system, the whole world, the whole human race, the whole history of error, failure, madness, and death. The whole business of legends, stories, dramas, religions, cities, embracings, buildings, roads, ships, music, dancing, surgery, print, paper, paint, sculpture, you name it, for whatever its name may be, *that* is what genius deals in, and with.

That is what genius wants to make straight, and to put in a bright light, corrected.

Well, of course, this *trying* is all we really have, the rest is even less than this, the rest is really nothing when the tallying is done, the rest is ash, dust, and the invisible slag heaps of error and loss as big as solar systems.

What these geniuses put forward is very little, compared with the potential, or with the original itself, all things already and for billions of years real and in place, but it is the only thing we have that is our own, that *we* have made, and after ourselves, after our continuous putting forward of ourselves, through the procedure invented or given as a gift by nature to *all* continuing things, after our most astonishing falling in with the procedure, our successful recreation of ourselves over billions of years, in all of our various forms, these things, this *art,* made by our madmen, our disgruntled boys, our violent girls, our geniuses, our refusers, our frequently sick boys and girls, these homemade things are all that we have, all that we call culture, civilization, and mortal glory.

Every man is correct in asking God why he is stuck with himself, and his rotten luck.

If he wasn't permitted to choose his parents, he should certainly have been permitted to choose the people he must have to deal with during his life, but this also is denied him.

He can neither choose his parents, nor choose not to be drafted into the Army, even, for instance.

2

EVERY PERSON in the world has a favorite person, and if he is a sensible person, or a lucky one, his favorite person is himself, even if he doesn't know that this is so, or knows it and pretends he doesn't, or swears on a stack of Bibles that it isn't so, because his favorite person is Jesus, for instance.

But it is also possible that there are very smart people, very intelligent people, very wise in the mystic ways of the mind and soul, and hip to the tricks of the inner man, and it is also possible that these people, either in addition to being their own favorites, or *instead* of, have a great kinship with somebody else.

Sometimes it is an animal, even, which of course to them *is* somebody else.

Well, just who is a dog? Well, a dog is the *owner,*

is he not? And the cat, who is the cat? Also, the owner. And the canary, who is the canary? Also, the owner. So again his favorite is himself, as D. H. Lawrence suggested long ago.

And how about the strange people whose pets are boa constrictors? It is the same with them, too.

And how about the people who have a child, or two children, or three, or four, or eight, or twelve? Who are *those* people, and who are their children?

Well, again it is the same, although with the children it is drawing nearer to what goes on in the human experience in relation to approval, acceptance, admiration of one person by another.

He is his own worst enemy, as they say, or, he is his own best friend.

Variations of these remarks are spoken all the time, suggesting that nobody is really fully integrated, and that one side quarrels with another, except in the case of the person who is enchanted with himself, whereupon everything is quite nice all around, as far as it goes.

Well, how far *does* it go?

The person who approves of himself, does he also approve of his father, mother, brother, sister, neighbor, friend, and the human race in general?

Yes, he does, sometimes, for in some approvers there is a force of energy that keeps moving out to everybody else.

But on the whole, the person who thinks very highly of himself, and is not really very much in any *real* sense, is liable to find fault with everybody else, and with the whole world, and with the whole human race in it.

Why?

Well, finding fault supports this approval of himself, this admiration for himself. When he carefully considers the genius of a great scientist, he decides that the man's achievement is actually an achievement of publicity, patronage, and favoritism, which compels him not to give up one iota of his admiration for himself.

Still, while self-approval thus is seen to be more often than not the mark of the nitwit, the fact remains that it is both desirable and necessary for every man in the world not to have contempt for himself, unless it is for the amusement of his friends, an act, a performance, and in reality a kind of superapproval of himself.

For if a man actually does not find it possible to regard himself at least with courtesy, he must be a rotter, and he must know it, and this places upon him the choice between ceasing to be a rotter so that he can have a courteous relationship with himself, and therefore with his parents, his tribe, and the rest of the human race, or choosing quite simply to cease to be, at all.

He can stop the rotter by a living effort, or he can stop him by killing him. It's as simple as that.

He can't be both and not be phony. But how amusing a phony can sometimes be, just so the phony doesn't happen to be your wife, for instance.

MOST OF ALL I cherish having met the two people
I had the good luck of meeting in the only way in which
a meeting may be truly considered a meeting: my son
Aram two hours after his birth in New York on Saturday September 25, 1943, and my daughter Lucy four
hours after her birth in San Francisco on Friday January 17, 1946.

Now, when you see a newborn human being, a new
life, as one might put it, and it is somewhat intimately
related to yourself, you are in fact seeing *something,*
you are in fact meeting *somebody,* and inexperienced as
I was when I first saw and met my son, I thought, "But
this fellow's *old,* he's older than any old man I've ever
seen."

And he seemed to be so intensely outraged that I

thought, "Ah, he doesn't like this at all, he doesn't like being in that little body, he liked it better where he had been. He's angry at his mother, his father, the human race, and everything else, because they've all ganged up on him and put him into that little body instead of letting him be everywhere, where he had been for so long."

And of course there is a *little* truth to this sort of thinking, because there is a little truth to *any* sort.

Soon enough, however, I began to meet him, when, even before he was a week old, he *wasn't* mad at me or anybody else. And I'm glad I *did* meet him, for such a meeting, a man meeting his son, even though even genetically it is now established that a son tends to inherit the character not of his father but rather of his father's mother's father's brother's son or something even more absurd and complicated than that—for such a meeting is a rather amazing event involving centuries of all manner of small and large accidents.

All the same, having had the first intimate connection with his arrival, the newcomer is both legally and physically indentified as being my son, and I was glad that he was, disregarding his own seeming annoyance, anger, outrage, which I was happy to notice had soon become a kind of secret amusement.

He was there. I met him soon after he arrived there. He was moving, he would grow, he would change, he would be a lot of trouble not so much to others as to himself, and so the Saroyan family would move along, the human race would keep going, both in faith and in ignorance, neither quite total.

And so it was. He fought it out and fought it out. He met a girl and married her and they have a daughter of themselves, so to put it. A poem about this child that my son published in the *Paris Review* in 1972 pleases me:

> little
> is what
> she is.

I like that. I like him. I like his wife. I especially like their daughter.

I met her when she was four months old. She was as serene as a sage. I liked that.

I am really glad I met my son.

And I am glad I met my daughter. But if I was confused by my son's appearance and attitude soon after he arrived, I was really surprised by my daughter's. As I told her when she began to ask about such things, when I first saw her, her face was all lopsided, perhaps because of the usage of certain birth-assisting metal instruments by the obstetrician.

Who knows? I certainly don't. When she was seven or eight years old, I told my daughter about herself at birth. She had been so ugly that, after pretending I was thrilled to see her, and walking down the hall at the Children's Hospital in San Francisco I thought, "Ah well, I guess she'll have a great mind, then. And perhaps be a writer."

After meeting your father and mother, meeting your son and daughter is the rounding out of that part of the human experience.

4

ALL LIVING THINGS have faces: lions, elephants, camels, whales, sharks, cows, sheep, frogs, tadpoles, eagles, tigers, antelope, canaries, mosquitoes, worms, butterflies, cats, mice, bats, dogs, and horses, to name only a haphazard few.

Well, the thing about people is that they frequently wear the faces that the other living things wear. Sometimes they even wear the faces of things that are *not* even members of the animal family. Everybody has seen somebody with a face that seems to be an apple, for instance.

In the human face the eyes are supreme, or so they say, but such sayings are now and then not quite supported by the facts. There are toads in which the eyes are too big to be readily acceptable, although all seemingly unacceptable things are soon seen to be not only acceptable but pleasing, for the simple reason that these things have been studied in relation to the whole creature, and in a toad pop eyes are quite appropriate, if not quite instantly appealing. But of course they are not appropriate in people, where they also occur.

The nose has a certain kind of importance in the matter of identity, for any man with a large nose has got to live accordingly, and we all know the touching story of Cyrano, as written by Edmund Rostand, who is said to have been an Armenian.

Who said so?

Several Armenians did, and with pride, too, adding, "Who else but an Armenian would write a play about a man with a big nose? No, sir, don't dispute the truth, Edmund Rostand is an Armenian, and if you insist I will explain how the name was made acceptable to France. Yedvard Rostomian, *that* was his name, or something *like* that, and with the wisdom of his race he changed it to Edmund Rostand, let us be pleased about this and not say he should never have changed his name."

There are many kinds of noses, and the people who have noses that are not quite perfect are forever regretting it, and thinking poorly of their parents, or at least of one of them. But even noses change. A nose like a spear in youth, in middle age becomes something more like a shield, and in old age a little bit of a thing that looks like a button.

At the outset I am proud to report two things: one,

that I have a nose that was very nearly perfect from the beginning, and Roman, in the classic sense, but was broken when struck by a baseball bat before I was eleven, broken again when I was twenty-two, and again when I was forty-four—the last two times in minor automobile accidents.

And twice the nose has been the object of surgical attention, both times by idiots who should have been rug peddlers, since the making of money was what they were really interested in.

And two, I am proud to report that like Edmund Rostand himself I am an Armenian. Again and again it is good to get such things clear at the outset. Therefore, the reader is invited to study his nose and to name his nationality.

I LIKE to go out every day and find a story.

Well, it's not quite that cut and dried, and if the truth is told I don't like to go out every day and find a story at all. I only like to go out, to go out. I can stay in and *choose* a story from out of a possible ten thousand stories always in my head, eyes, ears, nose, and throat.

If it is time to write, you have already *been* out, you have already found a story, at least one for every day of your life, possibly two, three, or four. Perhaps even a dozen stories for every day.

What is a story?

It's a writer with his mind made up to tell a story. To remember something, or to invent something. (It comes to the same thing.)

But something happened when I went out at three in the afternoon of the day after Easter.

I found my way up to Trinité and walked the full interior length of that old church.

I passed a businessman standing in a small alcove, staring at a hundred lighted candles. I couldn't even begin to guess what might be eating him, why he was standing there that way.

And last night I read the last chapter of *The Red and the Black* by Stendhal. In that chapter there was a lot of going to church and a lot of lighting of candles, but, then, that was in 1830, and this is 1972. What was a plain ordinary Paris businessman doing in Trinité, standing in front of burning candles, staring, and possibly even praying?

The fact is I found the whole situation in *The Red and the Black* just a little overearnest, and rather laughable, if the truth is told. And yet the book is considered both a classic and a monumental achievement.

Everybody in the story takes himself, and his ambition, and his busy little conniving mind, very seriously. The hero is a fatuous little bore.

I can't understand how he has won the sympathy of so many people for so long. They *do* identify with him, I understand, and when he goes to the guillotine for having fired two shots at a woman in a church, this very woman (who has been visiting him in jail and is madly in love with him) goes to his wife, who by law is in possession of his body and his severed head. She finds the wife kissing the lips of the head, an activity altogether out of order, very silly, and no proof at all of passion, love, helplessness, sorrow, despair, or even derangement—it's just a little bit of writing of some kind.

How long is the church going to have this hold over strange, unhappy, deceived, perfectly ordinary people—in novels, and out of them?

Well, after the short walk through Trinité, I went up Avenue Clichy past the Casino where Zizi Jeanmaire, the long-legged dancer, is the star—but in her theatre photographs she looks different, not the way she looked at a party in Hollywood twenty years ago. At the party she looked young and alive, but now it is all art, effort, control, and things like that.

Dogs everywhere, on leashes, tugging their people across streets to reach other dogs.

And so, up I went to the dealer in antiques on Rue Moncey to look into his window. Deadly, dear junk left orphan by the sudden death of the adoring owner, and now only for sale.

But where's the story I had gone out to find?

I was walking along Boulevard de Clichy, which divides the sex shops of Pigalle, when a man looking like a beaver came up quickly and said, "Vannik Vannikian from Beirut, I am a sculptor, I admire Henry Moore."

We stood and talked for five minutes, and *that's* the story, folks, let us please not make any more of it than that.

6

I AM PUZZLED by the people I once met, then forgot. And not *all* of them were met at parties, either.

The fact is I didn't go to a party until I was well along into adult life, as I believe it is put.

After my first book was published, one of the richest men in San Francisco, at the Family Club, where I was the haphazard guest of an architect, standing beside me, passing water into a porcelain work of sculpture, said joyfully, "Now, sir, where have you been all this time?"

For he did in fact believe that it was my fault that I had not met *him*, rich and famous and about sixty-six years old to my twenty-six.

So what did I reply?

Well, I don't remember, but I know it was nothing

clever, nothing at all proper or appropriate, and nothing to put him in his place, which he was quite neatly in, in any case.

I probably mumbled something like, "Oh, here and there," or, "Oh, out at 348 Carl Street, you know," or, "Away," which in a sense would have been true, for any man who puts in the required apprenticeship to become a professional writer must virtually take himself out of, and away from, all potential intrusions and instant distractions. One distraction would certainly have been hobnobbing with the rich, such as that old boy at the pissoire of the Family Club in San Francisco.

I never saw him again, although he went on another ten or twelve years. And I am still running into people I met for a moment ten years ago, or twenty, or thirty, or even forty or fifty. In other words, he's dead, but we did once stand side by side and pass water and words.

I suppose I feel sorry for the people I met but didn't remember because unless we *remember* people, they don't exist, and if anybody I have met doesn't exist, this is a terrible loss—to *me,* never mind what it may be, or not be, to him.

At the Aviation Club on the Champs-Elysées in 1959 I met a whole slew of gamblers, hustlers, hangers-on, con men, pimps, underworld characters, detectives, Corsican casino workers, Armenians, American blacks, African blacks, Asians, and a good variety of all-around international mothers.

I loaned money to anybody who put the bite on

me, but not one man came back of his own free will and paid the debt after he had gambled and won.

Now and then when I insisted on reminding such a gambler of the loan I had just made, he sometimes affected astonishment with himself for having such a weak memory and quickly paid back the loan.

But sometimes he asked was it one thousand francs I had loaned or was it *two* thousand, and when I said it was one *hundred* thousand, he said I must be mistaken, it was one thousand and he offered the appropriate piece of paper marked 1,000, which of course I told him to keep.

He sometimes said he had *not* borrowed from me, he had borrowed from Mr. Hestatin of Holland, he never borrowed from anybody excepting Mr. Hestatin of Holland, how could he have borrowed from me? And as for me, I had never heard of Mr. Hestatin, and to this day do not know if I have got even the spelling of his name right.

The reminded borrower sometimes paid the precise amount borrowed on demand, but he did so with such alacrity that I was *thereby* informed unmistakably that he had no time for a man who having made a small loan insisted on having it back, as if it were a law of some kind—if a law, then very well, here is a full *compliance* with that stingy, cheap, nagging law.

He sometimes said he would pay his debt but not now, for it was bad luck to pay a debt while he was winning. And then after another hour or two, after he had gone broke again, he did not consider it bad luck to come and ask if I would be so kind as to lend him another one hundred thousand francs—and walked away annoyed when I confessed that now I was broke, too. In short, by walking away he was letting me know that only a fool would lose his own money in a Corsican gambling house. And he had no time for fools.

I have forgotten people like these all my life, but as we see I have *not* forgotten them totally. I remember them as vague and dismal pieces of comic human behavior, and I feel sorry for them because they don't have faces.

SOMEBODY IS always telling somebody else to start at the beginning, and to tell precisely what happened without any ornamentation or elaboration, as if such things are ever *not* part of *exactly* what happened, especially in legal disputes.

And some lawyer who has gone to school tells a kind of poet who hasn't gone to school, "Now, Mr. Tutunjian, just tell us in your own words what happened on the morning of January 1st, 1919, when you got up in your house at 248 L Street between San Benito and Santa Clara Streets, at four minutes after four in the morning, and smelled smoke, what did you think, what did you do, just tell us *that,* and nothing more."

Whereupon the poet looks around in desperation as if to ask, "For God's sake, where did this lawyer come from? Everybody tells me to go to Mr. Chicken-hawk, so I go to Mr. Chickenhawk instead of to our own Khoren Kuyumjian, and this American lawyer tells everything, then he tells me to tell what he has just told, but he tells me to tell it in my own words, which are now not my own words at all, they are his."

Well, having had a lawyer in the family, Aram of Bitlis, I now and then heard about a case in court, and about the strange behavior of witnesses, of opposing lawyers, of judges, of members of juries. Thus, it was soon impossible not to notice that while everybody was obsessed with the idea of getting things straight, that was impossible. It *never* worked that way.

In fact the harder everybody tried to get things straight, the more things became entangled, impelling one Armenian who had lost a case in court to remark, "Well, it is now a matter of the knife."

But the idea is a good one. If it is possible to get something straight, that is a desirable thing.

Even more important than clarity in the *statement* of what happened, however, is clarity about the happening itself, which is not really possible, and the reason history is hilarious.

Even when an event has simplicity, the giving of an accurate account of it is very difficult, and your house on fire isn't anything at all like a simple event, but then nothing *really* is.

Mr. Tutunjian had been accused of arson, but his lawyer, Mr. Chickenhawk, had got him acquitted and was proud of that fact, considering he himself was never quite sure his client hadn't set fire to his house, but probably only as a consequence of having had in mind setting fire to the insurance company, in retaliation for not being honest with poetic illiterates.

8

THE RAGTAG, bobtail, odds and ends of people known for a short time linger in the memory, and this has always seemed to me an indication of the unaccountableness of identity, and of the action of mind and memory in a given conglomerate, which is a person.

For instance, I have never been able to understand the basis of memory's selectivity, if in fact memory may be said to have such a basis, if it is not all of it pretty much whimsical and possibly even mischievous.

The reality of the people very near in one's life—the family, in short—is a large reality, so of course one understandably remembers *them*.

But what about the stragglers everywhere and all the time, from the very beginning of one's memory?

Why is one straggler remembered and another forgotten?

There was a boy at Emerson School in the second grade who had a name that struck me as exceptional: Fay.

This boy now and then fell in beside me in the school grounds during recess, and without so much as saying a word began to be a friend.

He belonged to one or another of the Anglo-Saxon peoples, very poor, very earnest, and very decent.

One Saturday he came from wherever he lived to Armenian Town and found me in the empty lot next to the house at 2226 San Benito Avenue.

"I know where there's a catfish," he said softly.

Well, now, it must be understood that fish and game of any kind are goals of pursuit in the minds of all small boys: birds, rabbits, snakes, fish, anything alive, beautiful, and moving, capable of eluding capture, anything compelling pursuit but never willingly submitting to capture.

I say *willingly* because at Vahan Minasian's peach and apricot orchard called "Glorietta," a little northwest of Roeding Park, I had frequently climbed a stepladder very quietly to the nest in which sat a cooing dove, all soft and gray and beautiful—a magnificent achievement of form, design, and utility: a bird.

And I wanted to experience some of that magnificence.

I did not want to harm the bird, or to capture it as something to keep, or to cook and eat it, but I did want to reach out and touch it, and I felt that the bird ought not to resist that gesture. But invariably the bird *did,* and took to explosive, noisy flight, leaving four absolutely beautiful little eggs in the perfectly shaped bowl of the nest. And of course the eggs were *not* touched, for I had heard that once touched the mother dove would not, *could* not, accept them. This was puzzling, and even then not really believable, but on the chance that it might be true, I never touched the eggs or took them, as many kids did, for collections they were making.

I only wanted the bird to know I was a friend, and the next evening when I climbed the stepladder again, I hoped that it would *know* I was a friend and not overdramatize the situation by taking off with a lot of crazy speed and wing-clatter.

But my plan never worked and I learned my lesson. Birds don't traffic with people. Birds and people *see* one another but they don't share one another.

All the same there is a rather famous photograph of Grey of Fallodon with a small bird perched on his head. Coming out of the sky, this little thing had made a friend of the old man who had become almost blind, and the old man was very proud to have been chosen by the little bird. Such things *also* happen.

I said, "Where is the catfish?"

"Back of Sun Maid."

This meant back of the raisin packing house, about a mile south by east.

We walked, talking quietly as we went, but I don't

remember anything we said, although I am sure I asked a lot of questions about the details of the situation, which I soon saw for myself.

A ditch was going dry, and there *were* in fact fish of several kinds in the larger ponds of the ditch.

We *saw* the catfish, with its cat's whiskers, but we didn't catch it, wading after it and suddenly lunging for it. We were in that tree-shaded place about an hour, and I have never forgotten it.

That's all. But why did memory choose to preserve this event and not to preserve so many others?

HAVE I EVER known anybody who was an absolute delight to know? Well, no. And one questions if it is in fact in the nature of things for such a person to *exist,* in anything like an enduring way.

My daughter, however, before she was sixteen, and especially before she was six, absolutely stunned me every day by the simple beauty and sweetness of her truth.

I won't go into detail and try to explain it, because it can't be done, but I will say that she seemed to be outside the human race, a member of another race, and of course we know that such a thing is not possible.

But she was somebody else, as the saying is.

Her very breathing was something else. Breathing the same air, when *she* breathed it, the air became different. And it did different things for her than air does for others. Her voice, for instance, was beyond the human range. It was soft, and so extraordinarily moving that upon hearing it one didn't know what to do about it, to show one's total devotion to it, whatever it was that had made it so much another order of voice, so much another order of usage of human breath.

And even when this little body, containing the unknown and unknowable person who was both already totally real and being made slightly different every day and every *instant* of every day, was suddenly outraged by some kind of betrayal or unkindness directed upon herself by somebody else, a brother two years her senior, for instance, and the little body breathed more deeply and more quickly in order to shout red outrage, her voice was suddenly the voice of somebody who obviously *was* in the human family, but only apparently by some lucky mistake—lucky, that is, for the rest of us, especially me, the father.

Shouting threats and maledictions at the offender against her truth, the little girl was still an absolute delight, and I used to marvel at the mystery of the whole thing.

How does such a thing happen?

Well, if we don't know, it really doesn't matter too much, because in any case whatever it is that has happened, it fades away of itself, and behold, there before you suddenly stands a young lady of the world, of the *real* world, as they say. Of the real real *real* world, might be a fuller and more accurate way of putting it.

What happens to kids?

For I *am* implying that something of what I noticed in my daughter when she was very little must surely be noticed by other fathers in *their* daughters, and then the whole magical thing wisps away as if it were the flawless cosmology of a dandelion broken. The little pieces forming the miraculous circle of eternity lightly disengage themselves from one another, the design softly breaks, and that's the end of that part of the life and story of another little girl.

The thing that probably happens is the thing that has troubled so many poets who had a lot of talent but not much sense: the inevitable.

And this inevitable thing is certainly commonplace enough to deserve every bit of respect and concern that can be bestowed upon it.

Something like a leap of a billion years of accumulated experience takes place in the tiny body of a new arrival from outer space, so to put it.

She is now here, in person, totally, but she does not have the slightest memory of that other place, or *way,* or truth. And she does not have one piece of behavior from then and there, excepting possibly a low soft late afternoon sigh.

Yes, my little daughter was a delight to know, just as my little son was a fascination. Until each became a full member of the human race, by choice, by practice, by experience, by pose, by purpose, by fate, by law.

Well, of course, that is how it is done, how the world is kept alive, and how the human race remains human, and stupid—but also inexhaustibly charming in its folly, muddleheadedness, and pomposity.

Well, anybody else? A daughter and a son, *that's* more or less to be expected.

Anybody else, especially strangers?

Well, there *have* been many people known to me for only a very short time who might be said to have been altogether delightful—but the trick of it is that such people *were* known only a very short time. They weren't really who they seemed to be. They were fantastic and delightful for only *that* moment.

I WAS ESPECIALLY concerned about noticing carefully people who did things like draw or paint, for it
seemed to me that they were using a language which I
was not sure wasn't better than the language of words.

If somebody could play a musical instrument, I
was absolutely astonished and filled with admiration,
even if the instrument was only a ten-cent harmonica,
and the music was "Yankee Doodle."

It followed that I myself was favorably disposed
towards trying to make pictures with lines and paints,
or music with any kind of instrument I could buy for
a dime, for it was out of the question that I would have
a dollar to lay out for an authentic Hohner harmonica,
for instance, instead of a ten-cent imitation one, made
in some kind of madhouse factory in which imitations

of *everything* were made for quick sale, quick usage, and quick deterioration.

The pictures I made with lines were frequently pleasant to behold, especially the following day when I had forgotten what I had been trying for.

The painted pictures were also acceptable if I stuck to animals, houses, roads, and smoke, and didn't try to do ideas. I was quite good at making pictures of only colors and masses, which kids really *want* to do but are bullied into not doing by an unspoken admiration by adults for literalness.

Now, anybody knows that there are all kinds of amateur artists in every community in the world. These are people who make things that ordinarily can't be sold, for which there is no real measure by means of which to arrive at a value, and for which there is no demand.

A great artist of this kind in Fresno was a young dark fellow by the name of Sarkis Sumboulian, who used pen and ink in the making of pictures of great heroic castles at the top of great heights and among great roaring clouds. And he put rather good titles to these pictures: *Träumerei,* for instance. And so somebody would say, "What does that mean?" And he would say, " 'Träumerei' in German means dream."

Sarkis Sumboulian had drawn one more of his dreams. It had been inspired by the music of Schubert, but he himself in his little shack of a house on M Street in Armenian Town, sitting at the table after dinner while the rest of the family read papers or talked, slowly started a pen and ink drawing, and worked steadily for the next two or three hours, until it was finished. In an appropriate place at the bottom of the mighty picture he would write in fine letters: *Träumerei by Sarkis Sumboulian Fresno December 1918.*

At that time he was about twenty years old and out of school. A high school diploma was on the wall of the parlor in the little house, and he contributed to the family living costs by finding work either in a fruit packinghouse, in a department store, or in an office, doing stuff that anybody can do.

But he was an artist. He was not just *anybody.*

About once a week he finished a new drawing.

The paper cost about a penny a sheet and came in a book of fifty sheets, glued together at the top: after you finished a picture, you separated it from the tablet.

He generally took the picture straight to my father's kid brother Mihran, and together they looked at it for a long time.

Pipe organ pictures, I called them. There was deep in each of them a large bellowing approximation of a sorrowful moan.

Sarkis Sumboulian had a nervous breakdown, but he was *said* to have gone mad. At the age of twenty-four, he left town.

One day Mihran told me, "He's in London. Sarkis Sumboulian is in London, he is drawing pictures in

London, he sent me this letter in Armenian."

And that was it. I never found out what finally happened to Sarkis Sumboulian in London, or anywhere else. Maybe he only died.

I HAVE frequently *sung* Bitlis, for it is the highland city of my people, and in a sense a nation by itself, in which the three peoples living there side by side felt closer related to one another than to others of their own tribes in other cities: the Armenians, the Kurds, and the Turks.

I place the Armenians first because Bitlis is a part of ancient Armenia. I place the Kurds second because Bitlis has also been a part of the geography of the Kurdish people. And I place the Turks last because they were the last to arrive.

Now, when a great many of the Armenians of Bitlis saw that the future for them in Bitlis was at best only heroic, with violent death almost inevitable, the alternatives were carefully considered—to stay and die

Armenian, or to go to America and die old. Many Armenians voted to die old, and went to America: New York, Rhode Island, Massachusetts, Illinois, Michigan, and most of all to California, although there are Armenians in every state of the union, and in all probability in every country of the world.

This is quite a large fact when it is remembered that in 1915 there were scarcely three million Armenians in the world, counting half-Armenians and quarter-Armenians, a kind of counting that Armenians tend to do. It is never imagined that the English, German, Russian, Assyrian, Greek, French, Italian, Irish, Spanish, Portuguese, or American half will be *preferred* by the half-breed over the Armenian.

Now, in singing Bitlis I can only say I have been helpless, for that seems to be the truth.

Whenever I met somebody in Fresno whom I considered especially brilliant I immediately asked him to tell me his city, the city of his people, and more often than not I was told, "We are from Bitlis."

This always pleased me, and I thought, "Another member of the family."

One of the greatest characters in Fresno in the second, third, and fourth decade of this century was a large burly man with a huge open smiling face—the whole *face* smiled, not just the lips and eyes—whose name was Aram Joseph, which means that his full and proper name in Armenian was Aram Hovsepian.

He was one of the better local wrestlers, and was

frequently the headliner at the Friday night matches at the Civic Auditorium.

If the matches were fixed, nobody seems to have dared to ask Aram Joseph to lose, for he won every one of his matches. This was wise, for many of the ticket-buyers were Armenians, but not necessarily from Bitlis, for the people of Bitlis don't like to throw money around foolishly. That is something that is done by the less sensible people of Van, Moush, Sassoun, Dikrana-gert, and a dozen other Armenian cities.

Whenever Aram Joseph was scheduled to wrestle, he would hand out two or three dozen free passes to members of his own family, and to a number of other good friends, mostly from Bitlis. He had a blonde appearance, blue eyes, and a kind of early California style of movement: powerful, swift, loud, hearty, generous, and in a street fight deadly.

Selling papers, I saw him one day pick up and heave onto the sidewalk from a small real estate office in which he had a desk three very big Americans, as they were referred to in those days. If one of them got up and didn't run, Aram Joseph gave the poor man a clout with the edge of his hand upon the neck that sent him flying. Three big men, tough guys, the kind of characters who in television westerns these days would be regarded as killers. Aram Joseph ignored all threats upon his life until the moment it appeared to be in operation, whereupon he would take a pistol or a knife from somebody, knock him down and keep the weapon, which under the circumstances he was legally entitled to use upon the would-be assassin, but never did. But he did have a good assortment of weapons.

One day only a few years before he died, Aram Joseph stopped me on Eye Street in Fresno and said, "Willie, I want you to know your father was my teacher in Bitlis. Armenak Saroyan was the best man I have met in this world."

That was one of the proudest moments of my life.

One of the *funniest* was watching Aram Joseph back up a Kissel Kar three blocks on Van Ness Avenue at 60 miles an hour in 1919.

12

ON NINTH AVENUE in San Francisco between Irving and Judah Streets there used to be a cabinet-maker who lived above his shop. He was called in the old country manner, Barone Gapriel, or Mr. Gapriel. His family name was Jivarian, and he, also, was from Bitlis. He wrote poems.

I asked him how it happened that he took to the writing of poems, since he was a cabinetmaker, and a very good one.

He said, "Well, now, my boy, Mr. William, when I am standing here at my bench, doing my work, my mind does not have very much to do, it is a matter of hand, and eye, so my mind speaks to me, saying things, and pretty soon I listen to my mind. I hear my mind say one word, two words, one line, another line, and so in the evening after work I write down what my mind has told me. That is how it happened."

He was a man of medium height, heavy set, with something about him that suggested the trunk of a large tree. His shoulders were broad, his hands large, his fingers well shaped and very strong. His eyes had in them a mixture of terrible sorrow and continuous dancing amusement.

His kids were away at college, for that was the one thing he believed was his responsibility to them, to see that they were as well prepared for sensible living as anybody might be: two sons, one daughter. His wife he had found in America, but again she was from the city of Bitlis. Every afternoon around three she took him a brass tray, upon which rested a small cup of Turkish coffee, one piece of lokhoum, and a glass of cold water.

She smiled and said softly, "A moment of refreshment for you, sir."

She left the tray on a clear place of his workbench and went back upstairs, for she knew that when he was in his shop he was an artist, a thinker, and did not want any kind of small talk to intrude on his own cabinet-making and poetry-thinking.

Now, in those days there was a famine in the land, one might say in the manner of the writers of the Old Testament. There was certainly a shortage of money, and many poor families became poorer. All the same, they managed to sit down to hearty meals of very simple and very inexpensive fare, including my own family, in the second floor flat at 348 Carl Street, about eight blocks from the shop of Barone Gapriel Jivarian. I was twenty-two years old and felt just slightly desperate about not having a steady job. Also, about not having become a published writer, although I worked at writing every day, and pretty much also every night.

Thus, being without income and therefore also without cash, I did a lot of walking, and a lot of water drinking, until suppertime, when great mounds of bulghour pilaf cooked with cut-up brown onions was heaped upon plates, so that my brother and I could eat heartily if not elegantly, so to put it.

I loved the stuff, and I still do. And long after I was rich, I frequently asked somebody to cook a big pot of it for me, or I asked a chef at a restaurant to make a special big pot of it for the following day. And finally I myself learned how to fix the dish, and so I have it whenever I want it, wherever I happen to be.

On my walks I frequently passed the cabinet-maker's shop, and once or twice he saw me and waved at me to come in, whereupon he would say, "Well, now, you're just the man I want to see, Mr. William. You are a writer, although not yet famous. You use the English language. I, also, am a writer—well, perhaps not quite a writer, but at any rate I write my poems. And I use the Armenian language. This is the poem I wrote last night."

And then he would read a poem that I thought was wise and human, and incredible, not for a cabinetmaker to have written, but for any man to have written.

And I thanked him and went on to the beach

where I walked and picked up pebbles, as if they were words, or coins of money.

Four years later, I broke through at last, and my first book was published, let me even now, almost forty years later, say praise heaven, praise God, praise Jesus, praise the sun, praise everything and everybody. While the poems of the good cabinetmaker were never published, heaven help us one and all.

13

BUT EVERYBODY who is brilliant, or at any rate slightly more brilliantly *stupid* than other people, doesn't come from Bitlis, although the people who *do* come from Bitlis like to think that everybody who is brilliant *does* come from Bitlis, especially the big oafs, who are invariably eager to uphold the Bitlis tradition for superiority in all things, including loud vulgarity, and in this ambition are unfailingly successful.

The only trouble is that in the end one or another of the big oafs turns out to be really only a shadow less intelligent than the most enormously famous *intelligent* man in town, Armenian, Christian, infidel, or Anglo-Saxon.

My own branch of the Saroyan family has its share of both kinds, and I seem to represent a kind of combination of them: the wise man, and the fool, or at any rate the lunatic.

But it must be stated, so that it may be understood, that the word for lunatic in the Armenian language, *khent,* is used without scorn and in some cases with admiration, if not indeed even with reverence.

David of Sassoun was *khent,* for instance, and if you don't happen to know what he did, let me sum it up by saying that he did everything.

Not all of the great, exciting, or only moderately interesting people of Armenia come from Bitlis. Sassoun for instance is about forty miles slightly northwest of Bitlis, and there have always been some fascinating people in that mountainous city.

On the other hand, there are cities whose fame lies almost exclusively in the commercial talents of its people. These people are businessmen, merchants, shippers of precious merchandise, bankers, money lenders, building construction financiers, and rug merchants. And of course it is expected of such people that on the one hand they will be ruthless in their exploitation of people, including widows and children, and on the other hand that they will donate enormous sums of money to heroic charities. In their wills they arrange that their fortunes shall go for the establishment of Armenian Schools all over the world, with fresh milk provided for little children at all times.

My mother's father, Minas Saroyan, had a kid brother named Garabet who went to Istanbul (which was called Constantinople in those days) and got into so much trouble over Greek girls and insults directed to officers of the Turkish Navy that he was hustled out of town to avoid arrest, and then sent to America, arriving in Fresno sometime in 1898, the earliest Saroyan in America.

In 1918 he donated a large sum of money for the Armenian orphans, including possibly many blood relatives who did not even know they were Saroyans. When the everlasting collectors of such funds presented themselves to him in 1932, he said, "Didn't those orphans grow up?"

He was one of the people I am glad I knew. I was just a little surprised ten years ago, long after Garabet had been dead and buried and all but forgotten, that a number of members of my family, seeing me suddenly after a year or two, said, "Why, when you came in here, I could have sworn it was Uncle Garabet."

Well, yes, we do have the same forehead and moustache, at any rate.

One day after I had had two books published I walked past the cabinetmaker's shop on Ninth Avenue in San Francisco, and he asked me to come in. He lifted a sheet of lined paper covered with writing, and said, "This is a poem I wrote two weeks ago. I have been waiting for you to pass by, so I could read it to you. Each line begins with a special letter. We do that kind of poetry writing in Armenia, you know. We also use this system as a code for the sending of messages to our people wherever they may be. All of our poets wrote poems with concealed messages in them: Unite, Armenians. Fight, Armenians. And so on. Well, *this* poem's concealed message is your name. I hope you like it."

And he read the poem.

I was embarrassed of course, because it was not only about me, but about my father, Armenak, and my mother, Takoohi, and about Bitlis, and Fresno, and San Francisco, and America.

I thanked him, and I left the shop.

Years later I heard that he had had a nervous breakdown and had been put into a hospital. And finally I heard that he had died, but I was glad to learn that at least he had died at home, in the flat over the cabinetmaker's shop.

I suppose it figured that he would first have to go mad, and then die.

THE PEOPLE you like when you meet them and while you know them, and the people you remember fondly, are invariably people who have a sense of *comedy,* not just a sense of humor. They are a people who can make you laugh, who do so deliberately because they like to hear you laugh. They like to see you feeling amused enough to forget that you really feel terrible about the whole thing, as many people do, from the beginning to the end of their lives, outraged first because they have been born, and then outraged because they must die. And, of course, it is just such people, with an addiction to outrage, who most enjoy laughter, and who in turn are most effectively able to make others laugh.

All comedians are people who really deeply con-

sider the human experience not only a dirty trick perpe-
trated by a totally meaningless procedure of accidents,
but an unbearable ordeal every day, which can be made
tolerable only by mockery in one form or another. And
the comedian's method is to notice that *the joke* is
steadfast in everything, there is nothing in which the
joke is not centered, including (or especially) in all of
those things which are ordinarily, even to the comedians, plainly sacred.

Now, the comedians I am thinking of are not the
stand-up comedians of the world of entertainment, although I have known, and still know, many of these
comedians. I find many of them good to know, too,
although most of them are bores who, away from the
act they do in front of an audience which responds to
their work and thereby expresses approval of them,
which they need incessantly and abundantly, most of
the comedians, when they are away from their performance, when they are themselves, are intolerable ego-
maniacs, totally devoid of imagination. And they have
the most unbelievable and unbearable order of pomposity known to the human race.

They actually believe everybody knows them and
loves them, and some of them, as they approach eighty,
and as they move nearer to ninety, believe God has
directed the flowers to open in the morning to express
God's own love for them, and for the butterflies to come
flying directly to their noses, in another expression of
God's love.

These professional comedians aren't really members of the human race at all, if the truth is told: when they are great, they belong to the angels, and when they are sick, as most of them are, they belong to the apes.

The comedians I am thinking about are the comedians of the world, not of the stage.

These world comedians entertain their friends and their families, and they do it all the time. My own family has been full of them, but only the men have been great comedians, although my mother, Takoohi of Bitlis, daughter of Lucy and Minas Saroyan, and married to Armenak, son of Hripsime and Petros Saroyan (whose original name was Hovanessian and took the name of his stepfather), my mother had the greatest skill of mimicry, of impersonation, of caricature, I ever saw in action: every person she ever met she nailed instantly to his mark: in appearance, stance, movement, speech, silence, gesture, and quality.

It was great family entertainment to see her in action, and she went into action because she had to, it was fundamental with her to acknowledge the peculiar reality of everybody she met, or saw from a distance— or on the stage, or in movies or newsreels.

And while she enjoyed laughter and lightness of spirit, she deeply felt the sorrows of the human race, as revealed in herself, and in those members of it whom she knew, all her life.

Every now and then, she would look up from reading, and say to herself more than to anybody else, "How sad it is."

15

So MANY MEMBERS of my immediate family have been "touched," I hesitate to write about them for fear their children will feel that a family secret has been let out.

As for the remote branches of the family, they also have their mad people, but I don't know them very well, and they have managed somehow to keep the madness well within the confines of family privacy.

My father's side of the family is given to a kind of abstract sorrow that sooner or later impels any member to flip his lid, or to have a ferocious struggle in order not to do so. Almost everybody in the family is a fault-finder, beginning with God, who can be awfully unimpressive at times, and at others the kind of idiotic practical joker who in human terms would be instantly killed by those who have been his victims. After God, these Saroyan mad, or *khent,* quarrel with the human race, especially that branch of it which goes under the genetic, national, or cultural heading of Armenian.

And then the fault-finding comes home to the specific family within the body of that nation, the Saroyans. And then to that specific branch of the Saroyan family to which the brooding man belongs; and then to his father, that strange mixture of fool and nobleman; and then to his mother, that poor ignorant proud woman; and finally this fault-finding goes out to the animals of the fields, the birds of the trees, and to the fish of the sea.

Very seldom does it come home to the man himself, but when it does, watch out, that's all I can say, because then you have a man not only depressed but *violently* depressed. And what he wants is for everything to change—God, the human race, the Armenians, the Saroyans, and the miscellaneous large bodies of authority, such as the Supreme Court of the United States of America.

It was to that large body that my father's kid brother Mihran once wrote; or said he had written; or went to a lawyer, possibly Manouk Hampar, to ask that the lawyer write on his behalf. Wasn't it enough for a man to be honest and upright, did he also have to be deprived of the very faith in himself which finally is the only excuse for a man to go on living?

And on he would go, saying things that had no apparent meaning, but seemed reasonable to him, and possibly even to members of his immediate family, and perhaps even to Manouk Hampar, that great soul, who had a policy of hearing out all madmen, especially of the Saroyan family, knowing they were unwilling to go to a lawyer *in* the family, of whom there were two, one specializing in loud criminal law, the other in quiet business law, one an actor and world-winner, the other a money-seeking bore. After hearing out the mad Saroyan, Manouk Hampar would say, deliberately using English, "This matter is now under official advisement. That will be one dollar."

For he knew that no sick Saroyan would make himself sicker haggling over a legal fee of only one dollar, and also that it permitted the Saroyan to feel that the matter *was* indeed now at last in the works, and the world was going to know about this fellow's lonely agony.

And then going down the hall of the Bank of Italy building, built in 1917, the fault-finder would say to the walls, "There is a matter of honor in these things, and the man who does not act on behalf of honor—well, how can he consider himself a *real* humanitarian?"

In his office, the lawyer might perhaps think about a kind of report to make to the Supreme Court, simply for the amusement of it, to mention to his fellow lawyers at lunch at the Mayflower the following day. "Dear Supreme Court. My client, one Mihran Saroyan, has commissioned me to inform you that his head which is usually as hard as a rock has lately suffered a certain amount of softening, so that he feels you have discriminated against him in some mystic, secret and nefarious manner. Don't do that anymore. Yours truly: signed, Pastabon Pastabonian." Or, Lawyer of Lawyers.

16

CHANCE ACQUAINTANCES are sometimes the most memorable, for brief friendships have such definite starting and stopping points that they take on a quality of art, of a *whole* thing, which cannot be broken or spoiled. And of course a sort of spoiling is the one thing that seems to be inevitable in an enduring friendship—new aspects of the person become revealed, and that which one had believed to be the truth about a person must be revised. The whole reality of the person must be frequently reconsidered, and so instead of having the stability of art or anything like art there is a constant flux, a continuous procedure of change and surprise, which at its best, if both people are lucky, is far more appealing than art, for this is the stuff from which art is to be made, from which art is to be continuously enlarged and renewed.

An acquaintanceship, if all goes well, can linger in the memory like an appealing chord of music, while a friendship, or even a friendship that deteriorates into an enemyship, so to put it, is like a whole symphony, even if the music is frequently unacceptable, broken, loud, and in other ways painful to hear.

One encounters acquaintances endlessly, especially on one's travels.

There is always somebody on the train, ship, bus, or airplane, who wants to tell you his story, and in turn is willing to let you tell yours, and so you exchange roles as you listen and tell. If the duet works well, you say so long at the end of the ride, and you remember the occasion with a pleasant satisfaction with yourself and with this other person who was suddenly a part of your story and of yourself.

Now, if you play your cards right, and this acquaintance is a pretty girl or a handsome woman, you can risk trying to extend the chance meeting to a non-chance meeting, but the rules of this sort of thing, although unwritten and unstated, do not tend to even permit either party to *think* in terms of anything less than absolute purity, absolute impersonality, total awareness that each represents the whole human race at its courteous best.

You have been thrown together accidentally, total strangers, in order to pass along as if to Truth itself, or to God, or to Memory, or even to Yourself and to Your Family, the essence of your own story and reality. You are not there to acquire more story, to have more material to carry with the rest of the material that still hasn't been really understood, or certainly hasn't been used, and you are there anonymously.

The game does not work if you let the other acquaintance know your name or who the people are in your inner life.

What you share is a kind of gentility, sympathy, and charity, not so much for one another, not so much each of you for the other, but rather for the unnamed people in your lives who have been stupid, wrong, unfair, cruel, and altogether human.

And so while the carrier moves steadily toward where you are going, you speak to one another, and you say things you wouldn't say to any other people, and you know everything you say is understood and will not be used against you, and then when the carrier arrives you look at each other and smile, and say good-bye, good luck, and you move along, and that's it, and you aren't sorry that that's it, you are pleased that it is.

I have had many such acquaintances—literally hundreds, but I remember best going back to San Francisco from New York in January of the year 1929, after I had failed to take the big city by storm, after I had *not* started my career as a writer just twenty years old. I traveled chair car the whole distance and the whole time, about eight days, I believe it was, it might have been even longer. And then all of a sudden during the last two hours of that long train ride a little girl joined me in a sip of coffee from the Candy Butcher's urn in the corner of the parlor car, and we got to talking. She was married, she was pregnant, her husband was an office worker in Denver, they had no money, she was on her way home to her mother in San Francisco until he could get a proper one-room apartment, with bath and kitchenette, but she was in love with everything, especially the baby, and her husband, and life. And with me, as well, as I was in love with her. And I may say passionately if also totally impersonally.

17

AND OF COURSE there are always one's enemies.

Many thoughtful men have spoken about their enemies with contempt, with absolute hatred, but also now and then with admiration, and sometimes even with warmth, especially when speaking of friends who went sour. No enemy is so annoying as one who was a friend, or still is a friend, and there are many more of these than one would suspect.

The worst enemy is the one who knows you and knows what hurts you most, and if he also has skills that you do not have, your situation is not very good.

Lawyers have skills many people do not have, although there have been, and there are, lawyers who in spite of their skills are fair game to people without legal skills who nevertheless know how to make even a lawyer know fear, and how to make him suffer pain.

There was a lawyer in New York who was more nearly a café society personality than an office man, for he did legal work of various kinds for people who earned enormous incomes in show biz, as they themselves put it. They needed to know how to prevent the government from taking all of their annual money and going on an Asiatic war spree of one sort or another.

And this man, demonstrating to these people year after year a sure skill in not allowing the government to rob them of their money, became a very popular member of their crowd.

He knew everybody, and he knew me, but I didn't join his happy, bustling, busy friends, who in the very manner in which they greeted him exhibited their fondness for him, or should I say their fondness for his ability to prevent the government from stealing their money?

I was in fact only just able to conceal my contempt for him, and also for his clients, the brisk, bouncing bastards, all athrill by their success in show biz, all aglow by the love and applause of the common people, as they put it, all of them dismal frauds, for whom at the very most one's contempt can be tempered by a little amusement, and that's all.

And this lawyer wanted me to be just a little less hostile, because hostility was *his* business.

Among his clients, and friends, were a number of people whom I was unavoidably obliged to have dealings with for a while, like a wife, and sometimes it happened that, when I was with these people, he was summoned, and a group formed around a table in a bar, to sit and discuss with him both business and pleasure.

And everybody responded to the lawyer fondly, and I didn't.

And he didn't like that.

Furthermore, I didn't do what everybody else had done.

I didn't tell him, "Now, look, I think the tax collector's taking too big a chunk out of my income every year. I couldn't help overhearing since I am right here at this table what you just told Joe Haffamann about the way you saved him a fortune of money, as the saying is, last year. Do you suppose you could do the same thing for me?"

The main reason I didn't say anything of that sort is that I wasn't *interested* in forming a fake corporation, and I didn't have, and I wasn't earning, and I wasn't ever likely to earn the kind of money that would make forming such a corporation worthwhile. How much could the well-loved lawyer keep from the tax collector when my entire income for a year was only around ten thousand dollars? Sometimes even less? Ah, but with his know-how and friends, I would soon be earning ten or twenty times as much, wouldn't I? Even so, I wasn't even slightly interested. If I were, I would probably choose to go into counterfeiting U.S. currency.

And so there he was, and there I was, and there were his friends, some of whom I had unavoidable and desperate dealings with.

Finally, one day one of these friends brought a legal action against me for a lot of money, and her lawyer was this well-loved bouncing boy.

What happened was that we were all at a fashionable bar having a couple of drinks and somebody asked where I was stopping in New York on this visit, and I mentioned the hotel, and an hour later, two minutes after my arrival there, I answered a knock at the door, and a young man handed me a summons.

I examined it and telephoned the lawyer.

Yes, he said, his client *was* suing me for all that money.

"Well, this is ridiculous," I said. "If anybody ought to sue, it ought be me, but I *never* sue."

The lawyer said, "No, I've read the papers involved, and you will lose in court."

And after about four years of dragging on and on, I *did* lose.

As for the lawyer, he died. But what fun, what fun for him while he was *like* in show biz itself.

18

AND I'VE MET a great many writers, most of them unpublished, quite a few slightly published, and a handful actually published. And they are, all of them, a fascinating lot.

There was the Finn who wrote for the pulps in the early 1930s. I used to see him at the Turk Street Poker Club in San Francisco, but writers aren't really poker players, although they *are* gamblers.

Poker players cultivate not being gamblers, they cultivate not risking money, they wait for the nuts, as the saying is, and then they display ferocious bravery and bet everything they have, as if at last they had gone mad, bluffing, which is the way *a writer* interprets their behavior, and calls, and loses.

I can't even remember the Finn's name, was it

Larsen? Well, anyway he was a slim fellow, quiet,
slightly brooding, as one now and then notices that a
Finn is, and there was just a touch of comedy in him,
as when he would make a kind of wild and hysterical
gesture, as if to shove in his stack to a man with the
nuts, and the man would imagine for an instant that he
had made another killing, whereupon the Finn would
smile and throw away his cards.

And then there were the many writers who enjoyed drinking and eating, laughing and talking, singing
and dancing, especially at Izzy's on Pacific Street in San
Francisco in those same years, the 1930s—and what
years they were.

Well, weren't we all young, and wasn't it therefore
proper that the years should be glorious? What girls,
what sweet girls had come down to the big city from
villages and towns in Oregon and Washington, Mon-
tana and Idaho: and how we fed them but didn't marry
them because who needed it, who wanted to spoil the
fun?

One of the writers who used to come to Izzy's in
those days was a man of about twenty-six, about my
age, and like myself not yet published, although I was
about to be, my first book had been accepted, as the
saying is. And with him was always a slim flower-like
beauty from a village somewhere in Utah, probably a
Mormon girl. The whole saloon noticed her. Every man
noticed how rare a flower she was, and how wrong it
was for her to be going around with this rather pompous, stiff, pale, ineffectual, bloodless fellow who

couldn't jump and holler and sing and drink a dozen grappa fizzes and feel great, this Anglo-Saxon fraud of a man.

And so everybody was concerned about this flower of a girl and this fraud of a man, including myself, and everybody tried to understand why the little girl continued to stay with such a weird fish.

The second time he arrived at Izzy's with the girl, he said to me, "Can I speak to you a minute, please? I know you're wondering about Delfina and me. Well, please keep this to yourself. I met her at the bus station a month ago. She was broke, not very well, and homesick. I looked after her. The idea was to send her home as soon as I could raise the money. In the meantime, I developed a cough and was examined. The trouble is she was there at the time, and the doctor believing we were married told her I have cancer of the lungs, and at best I've got six months to live. I tried to force her to go home, but she just won't hear of it. She is going to look after me—to my dying day. Don't let this get around, but I know you like Delfina and I can see that she likes you, but look at it *this* way. I mean, what the hell."

Well, of course that was something else again, and the writer and his Delfina were treated by me with great warmth and courtesy ever after. But suddenly one day I wondered how had *everybody* found out what he had told me in confidence?

Six months later the writer and Delfina disappeared.

A year later, however, they were seen together at another bar, and then thirty years later I saw them in one of the most hidden-away bars I have ever visited in San Francisco, and for a flash we recognized one another. He was about to call out my name, and I was about to greet him, and *her*, but I decided, Ah no, let him be. That lie was the best writing he ever did, let him enjoy it in peace.

And who knows what he had told the girl to keep her devoted to him? Well, now, that *is* writing, isn't it? The dirty little coward, bespoiling a sweet shy wildflower like Delfina.

19

I HAVE HAD a policy all of my professional life to write about the people in my stories with the largest possible sympathy, large enough at any rate for them not to appear to be monsters, even when they had in *reality* been monsters. Some of the originals of the people in my stories I both hated and wanted to kill, precisely as St. George had killed the dragon.

There weren't a great many of them, however.

And there were quite a few people who had once *seemed* to be monsters who later on seemed to be ordinary, and even amusing.

I hated D. D. Davis, the Principal at Emerson School, for instance, and considered him both a monster and a fraud, for he was the man who stalked about in the halls, and looked mean. And he was the man the teachers continuously threatened me with, saying, "You behave now, or I'll send you to Mr. Davis."

And every time they *did* send me, he gave me a strapping with a leather belt.

Why shouldn't I hate him?

But as time went by, I let it go. He had eleven children. He and his wife never lost a child. Armenian husbands and wives with that many children always lost four or five, in between. He was just another big stupid fellow, and so I have no intention of hating D. D. Davis, dead at the age of eighty-eight these many years. Now, his boys and girls are parents, grandparents, and great-grandparents of surely enormous numbers of more boys and girls.

Let him rest in peace, a man who had no business having any connection with *any* school at all.

He was a big laugh when in front of a whole class whose teacher he had surprised by an unannounced visit, he got himself uncaught on the other side of his winter underwear by squatting, lifting suddenly, and kicking out a right leg.

Walter Huston used to do the same thing when he was standing with people who were talking big, and it invariably made me fall down with laughter, for hadn't I long ago seen old D. D. Davis do it, but in pure innocence, while Walter Huston did it as editorial comment, so to put it.

I once asked him about it, and he said, "Oh, that's a little something I noticed as a kid, and then there was a famous vaudeville act called Rosalinda and Harry, and Harry used to do that all the time standing and chatting with Rosalinda, who was of course absolutely gorgeous—and Harry never seemed to suspect that Rosalinda might consider it odd that he kept doing exercises while chatting with her."

In January of the year 1929, when I returned to San Francisco after four months in New York, the only living writer in San Francisco I had ever heard about had the name of Charles Caldwell Dobie. I looked him up in the phone book, dropped him a line, and he replied, asking me to visit his "office" on Montgomery Street in a building I came to know years later as the Monkey Block, which was its nickname.

He had a cubbyhole containing a bare table containing an enormous typewriter.

He himself was a rather clerkish-looking man of perhaps forty-four to my twenty:

"*This* is a writer?" I thought.

And he said, "Now, what seems to be the problem?"

Well, of course, this just wouldn't do at all, but I decided to be polite at any rate, so I said, "Well, I'm a writer, and I wanted to ask another writer, 'Does it *help* if a writer *is* a writer?' I'm doing other work for a living, but I don't like doing that work instead of writing. That's all."

He studied me a moment, and then spoke rather kindly.

He's been dead now forty years or more, I suppose. He died young enough, but not nearly famous enough, and he did answer my letter and speak kindly to me. I honor therefore Charles Caldwell Dobie.

THE BEST that can be said for anybody is probably that you misunderstood him favorably. I don't believe you can say you understood him favorably. In short, the best that can be said of anybody is probably the consequence of a favorable misunderstanding. Some people, frequently scoundrels, are impossible not to like, for some reason, and this reason isn't based upon their corruption, or their corruptibility, their easy proneness to being diminished from a potential virtue to a demonstrated vice. It is something else, entirely.

One of my friends in Fresno was a dark boy called Rum, for Rustom, although nobody but the immediate members of his family knew his name was in fact Rustom, a name famous in Persian lyric poetry. He was a sturdy Armenian boy from big, strong, hearty parents.

He was the boy who in a recess fight with me did not understand that my striking him *only* on the shoulder was deliberate, so that I would not commit the offense of striking another human being in the face. But this big idiot, a man I could have destroyed, did what all big idiots in all areas of human activity do when given quarter. He accepted and gave none in return, but proceeded to strike *me* in the face.

I was outraged and astonished, not to say hurt, and would perhaps have had to lay into him in the same manner, which I really didn't want to do, had not one of the teachers in the schoolgrounds, a Mr. Cagney, flushed of face and outraged by what he had seen, stopped the fight, to tell *me,* rather than Rum, that I had no business getting into a fight with anybody, on *any* account.

Rum, being the idiot he was, gloried in the fine showing he thought he had made, smirking and pretending not to need to listen to this rather sissy teacher: what kind of a man is it who teaches the fourth grade at Emerson School, where all of the other teachers are women?

One of my best friends came to me after the breakup and said, "For God's sake, why didn't you hit him in the mouth? Why did you keep hitting him on the shoulders and arms?—your jaw is swelling up. Are you crazy?"

And of course I didn't quite know how to tell this friend, *not* an Armenian, an American, well, almost an American, a son of Irish people, as a matter of fact, I didn't know how to tell him I refused to hit another person in the face.

Now, the way the world goes is amusing.

The scene changes from the playground at Emerson School in Fresno to the Barrel House on Third Street in San Francisco. Rum and I are now twenty-one or twenty-two years old, and Fresno is far in the past, forgotten almost, and even our little fight is forgotten, almost.

He sees me at a table playing rummy for money. After the hand, I quit the game and have a beer with him at the bar, and we begin to meet there, or at the Kentucky just down the street, or at Breen's across the street, and to loaf around together in San Francisco.

Well, I had always known that Rum was an idiot, for it was a fact, but I rather liked him just the same, believing that since he didn't know he was an idiot, didn't even suspect that he *might* be, he was innocent.

But as I came to know him and learned a little more about him, I found out that he was also a pimp, that he pretended to be legally married to each of his girls, of whom he had had about half a dozen every year, and had sold them to other pimps, or to houses. And yet I did not drop him, or avoid him. We went right on being old friends from Fresno, loafing around together in the Tenderloin of San Francisco: until the world changed and I got drafted and he didn't, and years later I heard he had died, that's all.

21

I HAVE frequently misunderstood things. Forgetting everything I had learned from so much painful experience, I have stood years later in dumb disbelief, remembering, and laughed at myself, and wondered.

Lord, why have I always been such a fool? Is this true of everybody, or is it that you have chosen me for the honor? If so, why? Because I have a natural aptitude? Or as a lesson? If a lesson, what is it that you want me to learn?

But who can speak to God, or rather who *can't?* The question is, who can get an answer? Or at any rate an answer that isn't from himself?

Here, now I stand and laugh at myself, because I find that I can't think of anybody whom I have ever been half-enchanted to meet. I have surely met, one by one, at least a million people, for I am in my sixty-fourth year, so why am I still unable to choose one?

What am I waiting for? Am I afraid I am going to run out of people to write about? Write about Henry Miller, one of the most successful producers of fashionable plays on Broadway. I met him just as he was starting his decline, and we sat at a table in 21 with his old pal George Jean Nathan. And we talked about the New York theatre, and the theatre in London, and I told him about the real theatre, the theatre inside the home of every family, especially every American family.

Or if you don't want to write about *that* cheerful gentleman, why not write about Bennett Cerf, he was the publisher of your first book. Say a few kind words about a man who got a lot done in the way of moving from one place to another every day of his life, and at the same time amassed a fortune of—well, let's say eight cool million mother dollars, and let it go at that. Some of this fortune was made by joke books he had other publishers bring out. Each of these books was a best-seller and made big money both for the publisher and for the collector of jokes, for that is what Bennett Cerf was, as well as a maker of puns.

When we did a little loafing around together in New York in 1935 on my way to, and upon my return from, my first visit to Europe, he did so many puns that I finally said, "Hasn't any friend of yours ever told you that if you make another pun he is going to kill you?" To which Bennett Cerf replied, "*Everyone* has, friends and enemies alike." Only he put the reply into a pun, which I thank God I cannot remember.

Well, why not write about Bennett Cerf?

Well, I don't want to.

All right, write about somebody who isn't famous, or somebody who didn't make eight million dollars.

All right, I'll write about a young man standing in the entrance to a vacant store on Market Street in San Francisco in 1929, selling a book about the mysteries of the universe.

He had the mightiest mouth I had ever seen: it was tireless in its muscular action, so that everything he *said* was also *performed,* by his mouth. My brother Henry, standing with me to hear his whole pitch, about four minutes in duration, said, "Let's go back and watch him again."

He didn't say *hear* him, he said watch him.

And the second time, he was even better, but we didn't buy the book, although it was only twenty-five cents, reduced from one dollar.

22

I HAVE never known a great many first-rate writers, not even after I became published, but I have known a few.

I think I have always known more painters than writers.

There is something about a painter that I find not easy to understand. They almost invariably try to explain themselves, and they almost never are any good at it. They make a mess of what is in the painting, in its own language, which does not need any word of explanation at all.

Now, when I lived at 348 Carl Street in San Francisco and was twenty-four years of age and still writing and not selling anything, it came to pass that my brother Henry during a walk one evening after a big supper of bulghour pilaf said, "Right there in that house is a woman who works at Western Union, and she says her son is a great painter, shall we stop and say hello?"

So we did. The lady was a southern lady, and spoke a little like all of the southern ladies in so many of the southern novels, and movies, and plays, but not *all* of them.

Her manner seemed to suggest that she knew she was making quite an impression by her manner of speech, along the lines of the southern tradition, and she wanted to know, silently of course, if Henry and I appreciated her performance.

Well, I didn't know about Henry, but I really enjoyed hearing her, and for that matter *seeing* her.

Instead of being a slim matronly prim woman, she was large, overweight, warm, and given to ripples of pleasant laughter every ten or fifteen seconds.

"Well, now," she said, "you young men of ideas, like my own boy, Claiborne—he's a baby, my dear, only twenty-four, and how old are you?—twenty-four, too, how nice it is, you must stay and meet him, he will be home very soon, I'm sure you're not here to meet me and hear me rattle on and on, so just let me see that you are comfortable and I'll go fetch refreshment, I'll do my best, and I have an idea you will be perfect gentlemen and adore it, or at any rate *say* so."

She disappeared into the kitchen, and after a moment a very young man came out of there, and I said, "Are you Claiborne?"

And the boy said, "No, *he's* twenty-four, I'm eighteen, I'm Farragut, my mother just kicked me out of the kitchen."

After we had introduced ourselves, we asked Farragut about his brother Claiborne, and Farragut said, "Well, I can't say for sure, but it seems to me he must be some kind of wonder of the world, for he can look at somebody and look at him and start drawing and then painting, and after a while you will see *that* man on the canvas, and he will have something *more* in his face than anybody except Claiborne ever saw."

I was now more interested than ever both in meeting Claiborne and in having him let us look at some of his work, which his mother had assured us he would do, but which *she* herself absolutely would not do, as it would be sacrilegious.

Was there any *real* justification for the astonishment in the mother and brother about Claiborne's talent, whatever it might turn out to be?

At length the refreshment came out on a big metal tray: orange pekoe tea with lemon, gingerbread baked in the shape of little people, and cucumber sandwiches on very soft white bread without crusts.

I had a good go at the stuff, eating much more than my share, but as there was an enormous amount of it, and Henry ate only one of each, and Farragut only drank tea, it wasn't possible to notice how much I put away, unless you made a point of it, which I did. Four gingerbread people, eight cucumber sandwiches.

Then, at last, into the parlor came Claiborne himself, a sober, lean, rather touching figure of a young man, who immediately after the introduction said softly, "Would you sit for me, I'd like to try to paint you?"

And so I sat for Claiborne Tattersall twice a week for four weeks, whereupon he gave up.

"You're different every day, I swear."

Later, I heard he'd had a nervous breakdown. And at the time of the national draft I heard he was a conscientious objector and was put in jail.

But not everybody I ever met had a nervous breakdown, or was a conscientious objector.

23

A NEIGHBORHOOD has a kind of mystical identity which one scarcely suspects let alone notices while one is living there, for living uses up all of a man's time and attention. But in retrospect sooner or later a man remembers an old neighborhood and suddenly notices that there was something fantastic about the place.

Well, the neighborhood just south and east of Emerson School in Fresno was instantly recognized as an Armenian neighborhood, even though Syrians, Assyrians, Slovenians, Portuguese, Irish, and Serbs also lived there, and just at the edge of Armenian Town there was a Basque hotel, complete with a jai alai court. The Basques were shepherds come to the San Joaquin Valley to earn enough money in four or five years to go home rich, buy a farm, take a wife, and raise a family.

They did not tend to marry in Fresno. There was a continuous arrival and departure of shepherds at and from the Yturria Hotel near the Santa Fe depot. In town for a week or two, they sat and ate the hearty meals that came with the rooms they rented, gossiped, sang Basque songs, and availed themselves of the professional women.

One did not see a Basque boy or girl at school, but sooner or later, as all such things must, it happened. Many Basques did *not* go home rich, they stayed in California poor, or comparatively poor. And then some stayed rich, and others became very rich. And they took wives, and brought up families. Most of them took Basque wives, although quite a few took women of the region, of many nationalities.

Now, it may be impossible not to notice that the people who lived in Armenian Town were all members of other small nations. It may be fancied that my own high regard for these people, especially for the Irish and the Portuguese, was the consequence of Ireland and Portugal being small nations, but that is probably not the explanation.

I liked all of these people because they were quite simply part of the mystery of my neighborhood, because I saw them daily for quite a few years, and because they had a quality about them that both amazed and amused me.

Now, in the rest of Fresno, I knew members of other nationalities: Italians, Greeks, Germans, Danes, Swedes, Chinese, Japanese, Hindus, Mexicans, American Indians, and a few Blacks, apparently not from the South, however—probably from places like San Francisco, Portland, and Seattle—that is, people without a southern accent.

The sons of not all of these people came to the press room of the *Fresno Evening Herald* to take papers and to run to town with them to sell them, many of the sons of such people came to the *Herald* just to be with friends, to visit, as it were, and now and then one or two of them tried selling papers but soon grew tired of it and dropped out.

The only real hustlers of newspapers, the only real headline hollerers were indeed Armenians and Italians. They meant business, and the money they earned was needed at home, both to keep families going, and to enable these families to save money enough to make down payments on homes of their own.

There were others who regularly sold papers, but just a few of each: Greeks, Germans, and Americans.

Years after the neighborhood lost its identity and was as good as gone forever, I suddenly understood its mystery—it had been populated by willing exiles who nevertheless had deeply longed for a place they knew they would never see again.

24

THE PEOPLE you hate, well, this is the question about such people: why do you hate them?

Invariably the answer is this: because they were rude, they hurt your feelings, they hurt you, they tried to make you feel worthless, they nearly destroyed the self you had been working on for so long, they drove you to a kind of desperation.

Don't bully me anymore, old buddy, don't stand in my way, don't call me names, don't threaten me, I'm here, I'm moving, I'm not going to be stopped by you, so here I come, and if you try to stop me I'm not going to let you stop me.

This began very early in my story, in the streets of Fresno. It took the form of fights with other newsboys, or with boys of the streets. I had set out to be decent with everybody, but I soon noticed that if I was decent, this was interpreted as weakness, and somebody would decide to exploit my reluctance to stand fast, my willingness to move *around* the opposition. But doing this so deeply annoyed and humiliated me that when the bully arrived again, to continue the game, I said, "All right, fight, then." And stood fast, with clenched fists, and waited for him to come in, but he didn't, he was afraid to come in, he *wanted* to be tough, but he *didn't* want to get hurt, and he went away.

And so, soon again I became decent, and was aware of another's struggle inside himself, but sure enough was exploited again. This time, however, I didn't permit any humiliation to make me red in the face, but said, "I think you want a fight—well, I'm ready."

After a year or two of that, it almost never happened that anybody—boy or adult—misunderstood my preference to be decent with everybody. And I was not obliged to try to be some kind of tough guy who had no time for such sissy things as civility and goodwill.

But of course I've told it at least partly wrong, and in my favor, for to this day I am very easily willing to keep silent and to walk around what looks like totally meaningless, useless, ridiculous trouble. Don't hate—ignore. Don't kill—live and let live.

25

UP AT NUMBER 4 bis Rue Chateaudun four blocks from my four-room flat on Rue Taitbout, is a small square room on the street, which is a shoemaker's shop, not far from the entrance to a hotel with a name like Baltic. This hotel, according to a conscientious objector who did a little time in a pen somewhere in the United States for that private bravery, during the year 1944 was also a whorehouse, because he and his bride on their honeymoon took a room there, and the first thing they noticed was that there were a lot of men coming in and going out of the place, especially from 10 P.M. to 2 A.M., especially to and from the first and second floors, which in America would be the second and third floors.

In this little shoemaker's shop, which has a high ceiling and a steep corkscrew metal stairway that goes to a basement precisely the same size and shape as the shop, there is a large brown owl.

This bird has the freedom of the shop, the door of which is sometimes kept open on the street, and yet the owl has never ventured out of the shop.

There is no telling (by me) why *this* is so, but I do know the story, however sketchily, of the owl and its adjustment to life in the shoeshop.

A nice lady back from the country, whose apartment is two doors from the shoemaker's shop, brought into the shop one morning eight years ago two helpless infant owl chicks, both apparently near death.

She asked the shoemaker if he understood such birds.

He didn't, he said, but he suggested that she improvise a system of feeding them and keeping them warm. She in turn insisted that he keep one of the chicks for himself.

He did.

And that's how he has had the owl these eight years. And that's why the owl loves him, and he loves the owl.

His wife died recently, and his son and his daughter are adults, and well along into their own lives.

The shoemaker is a year or two younger than myself, he's sixty-one or sixty-two years old. He is an Armenian, born in Gultik, down from the highlands of Bitlis, but he was taken early in life to Antakya, which is the modern name for Antioch, where St. Paul stopped now and then on his missionary excursions.

Well, now, this man, Hovaness Shoghikian by name, is perhaps an inch or two under five feet in height, but powerfully built. As a matter of fact he was once a champion weight lifter and wrestler, and has many old photographs to prove it.

In short, he is not simply a shoemaker, although he actually *makes* shoes, *entire* shoes, and for forty years has never worn a pair of shoes he hasn't made.

First, it is his trade, and he likes to work at his trade, but nowadays almost nobody wants a pair of shoes made to order, to fit the feet, to fit a cast of the foot's precise shape. Second, his own feet are small and broad, and the best he has ever been able to do in finding a ready-made pair of shoes (before he began to make his own shoes) was not very good. Ready-made shoes were always something his feet could barely tolerate. But in his own shoes his feet are at home, and standing on his feet in his shop he himself is at home. Naturalists have visited his shop to speak with him about the owl, and about a green bird the shoemaker has had almost thirty years. "She can't grip with her claws properly," he says of the green bird. "But she will live most likely another thirty years, they sometimes live to be eighty."

Where he found out such a thing I can't imagine, for he does not look into books for information.

Without any outside help, or instructions, he long ago discovered that the owl has to have in its diet fur or feathers, otherwise its digestive procedure becomes impaired. And so all these years the owl has been fed thin strips of raw beef, chicken hearts, and live mice, which he buys from people who telephone to let him know there is a mouse in their trap.

And so of course the shoemaker loves the owl and the owl loves him.

The owl certainly permits itself to be held by the shoemaker. The two of them have a simple ritual of displaying trust and affection, which involves his saying, in Armenian, "Well, a kiss, then." Whereupon the owl puts its beak to his upper lip.

WHEN I WENT to work at the age of twenty-one
in San Francisco at the Cypress Lawn Cemetery Company, with offices on the eighth floor of the building that
stood and still stands on the southeast corner of Market
and Seventh Streets, a building bearing the name of
Hewes, which in one of my short stories I gave a better
name, Gravity—when I went to work in those offices,
for that firm, I discovered that the operation was a
family one. The biggest and easiest jobs were held by
members of a family named Johnson, but every member
had a rather fanciful first name. The top man was
called, for instance, Noble Johnson, and the name
seemed perfectly right for him, so that almost instantly
it was no trouble at all for me to accept it.

He was in his early thirties, but Noble Johnson

isn't the man I want to remember. My man is the *vice*-president, a man who had started at the bottom in 1889, and there we were in 1929—forty years later.

He wore black. He was skinny, he had long fingers, he had a long nose, and he liked to talk things over with people who worked with him, especially new people, and so it happened that when I applied for the job he said, "Now, you've come here for the job, and I'm in charge of hiring and firing, so let's get right down to business."

Whereupon he considered my name, age, address, family, nationality, religion, education, wealth, and finally, he asked the key question: "Do you want to make the cemetery business your life work, as I did forty years ago?"

To which I quickly replied, "Yes, sir, I would really like to do what you did."

Well, I got the job, of course. It was easy work, and every day I saw Noble Johnson come in for an hour, and go away. And every day I saw the Jolly Undertaker, as I came to think of the vice-president, come in and stay long after everybody else had gone home.

And every day I heard him mumble and hum to himself a song that Jimmy Durante had made famous: "Inka dinka do, a dinka dink adinko do. That means that I love you."

Well, how could a man so skinny and dry and pompous also enjoy the comic and wild *spirit* of that song?

He *had* to be somebody special deep down inside, I decided. And he was.

He wrote slogans for the cemetery, although Noble Johnson ruled them out one by one, and wouldn't allow them to be put on signs or posters or into ads: INTER HERE. Best of all: CYPRESS LAWN CEMETERY: WE GIVE YOU A LOT FOR YOUR MONEY.

He averaged one good slogan a week. I used to remember them, but everything goes in time, and so of course the old boy himself went, he's buried right there, free of charge, for faithful service.

I liked *that* old stuffed shirt, but I didn't make the cemetery business my life work. (Or did I?)

When I quit after a month, he was terribly disappointed, a young fellow who had started out like a son.

27

MY EARLY DAYS in San Francisco might be called the Bohemian Days, since so many of the young people I knew were addicted to art, and were working to achieve success as writers, poets, playwrights, painters, composers, sculptors, or all-around frauds, living on the fat of the land.

Everybody had something going, and there were a good two dozen of us who met fairly regularly, although by accident. Among these regulars for almost a year there was a strange young woman who gave a first impression of irresistible charm. Soon enough, she revealed more of herself, however, whereupon every man who had imagined he might want to know her more deeply, withdrew, some in astonishment, some in anger, and some with sympathy and courtesy.

Her full name suggested social solidity, and perhaps even family wealth, if not importance.

She certainly had a job in public relations or something at the Legion of Honor Museum, and wrote pieces for all of the papers, but preferred the *Call-Bulletin,* an afternoon newspaper, long since defunct, perhaps because the city editor was Scoop Gleason, who was supposed to be in the romantic tradition of the great American newspaper editors. Ruthless, that is, and always able to get a better story quicker and more dramatically than any of the editors of the competing newspapers of which at that time, in the early 1930s, there were four, although one of them was a half-brother the *Examiner,* which was the main Hearst paper of San Francisco.

On her own, however, whenever possible she went out and tried to hustle up a story that would make a hit with Scoop Gleason, if not with Dr. Walter Heil, her proper boss and the administrator of the Legion of Honor Museum.

She wrote a pretty good mood piece, as she put it, about retired old Italian men playing dominoes in a little coffee shop, who became so caught up in old rivalries brought from Naples that frequently two of them would have to be stopped from trying to strangle one another—and after half an hour of walking in the neighborhood, they would go back to the coffee shop and start a new game.

"I mean," she said, "I had no idea such behavior was possible. It certainly isn't in my family. When we

get murderous, we mean it. I have a kid brother somewhere in the world who left home after a fight with my
father ten years ago, and he was only sixteen at the time.
And my father is still just as mad at him as he ever
was."

The thing about this girl was a strange and instantly appealing beauty—of figure, complexion, and
body style. She looked as if all of her being was open
to being challenged, and right now, as it were, which of
course made every man upon seeing her for the first
time think, "Look at that." And then say to somebody,
"Who is that, pray tell?"

She herself, on the other hand, wanted only to be
somebody active in the arts, and writing was the area
she felt she might be able to manage. Eventually short
stories like those of Katherine Mansfield, and after that
possibly novels like those of Willa Cather.

Thus, she and I sometimes used to sit and drink
beer and talk, and of course while we talked she revealed more and more of her truth, which was at the
very least odd—she had strange fears, for instance.

She was sure one night soon a black man was going
to break into her bedroom, whereupon she was going
to pass out cold, from terror, and wake up sometime
later, and need a moment or two to remember what had
happened, to be terrified all over again, to run to the
door and lock it, and then to find a note scribbled by
the man, reading something like, "Oh, lady, you were
wonderful, so I didn't take anything else." And a few
months later she was going to discover that she was

pregnant. And she was not going to know what to do. Being Catholic she couldn't get an abortion. She certainly couldn't tell her mother or her father. She would either have to kill herself or have the child.

Well, she had two or three fears of that *kind,* and, as she told them, terrible things happened to her beauty, putting off any ideas any man might have about engaging her in sex.

28

IN 1959, IN PARIS, soon after I left my house on the beach at 24848 Malibu Road—the very number won my heart when I saw the FOR SALE sign on the house —and also left my room, 1015, not as good as 24848, but whatever the room lacked in numerological appeal, it made up for in size and height of ceiling, hall, and pantry, room 1015 at the Royalton Hotel at 44 West 44th Street, in New York, also a marvelous number, 44 West 44th, and had taken an Italian ship to Venice, with stops first at Lisbon, for a walk in the city, full of memories of where my kids and I had walked only two years earlier, and then in Sicily, in the westernmost town, whose name I keep forgetting, Messina is the easternmost town and I never forget Messina— Palermo, Palermo, that's the name of the westernmost town—and a stop in Naples, walks in each of these towns, and a stop in Patras, not far from Missolonghi where Byron gave up the ghost theoretically fighting for the Greeks in another of their losing wars with the Turks, but who knows about Byron, about legends, about death, and then on up to Venice, where I left the ship, and after a few gondola rides here and there, took a train to Belgrade, and bought a little car there—what is all this, why don't I get to the point?

Because, whoever you are, the point is that getting to the point is quite a problem of travel, and if you are going to get to the point, or even if you are only going to hope to get to it, you have got to travel, and that's what I'm doing. I paid $1,400 cash for the car with the German motor and the Italian body, and I drove, and drove, and stopped in Cannes, and began to gamble, and pretty soon all my money was gone. I was flat broke, a good $12,000 was gone, and I owed the tax collector back in Washington, D.C., $50,000, so what was happening?

I drove up to Paris, and noticed that now the month was April. April, 1959. (And that makes it precisely thirteen years ago, as I write.)

The going was bad, I was living the life of a millionaire, I ate caviar and drank vodka, I stopped at the George V Hotel, I gambled at the Aviation Club, I spent money, I lost money.

Finally, I went to work, to see about making up what I had lost, and of course going to work for me means sitting and writing.

And I made it, I got out of that time and trouble, I finished the work I agreed to do for money, and I got the money, and I began to pay off the tax collector.

On the leftover money I began to live. I rented a great place to which to bring my kids for the summer, but before they arrived in June, *late* in June I think it was, I had become a regular habitué of the Aviation Club at 101 Champs-Elysées, a *baccarat* and *chemin de fer* gambling club, and being the kind of gambler I am, I knew everybody, and everybody knew me. This is not a great achievement. The fact is it is no achievement at all. It is unavoidable at a gambling house that very soon you will know all of the regular habitués. And you will notice the arrival of newcomers, and their departure, generally in disarray and despair.

Among the regulars were Djingo, from Morocco, and Sergius, from Niger, whose mother was Turkish, he said, whose father was one of the biggest men in Niger politics. Sergius took automobile trips to Amsterdam now and then, and the theory was that he had added diamond smuggling to his other smuggling. But he never seemed to have money for gambling, or at any rate for what I call gambling, although he would take a place in the *chemin de fer* game and wait for the box to reach him, bet the equivalent of two or four dollars and hope to make four straight passes, and thereby to have suddenly: two makes it four, makes it eight, makes it sixteen, makes it thirty-two dollars. I once hollered at him, "Go again, you'll win." He went again and he won, and had sixty-four dollars for two, and passed the box, a thrilled man.

I liked Sergius and his pal Djingo, because whenever they saw me they smiled so dishonestly and disreputably that I had to bust out laughing: whereupon their own laughter became the most comic sound anybody ever heard—the sound of absolutely pure and authentic irresponsibility.

29

KNOWING ABOUT famous people, but never meeting them, that is something people who *aren't* famous
know about, and then if anybody ever meets a famous
person, or an *especially* famous person, it is a strange
kind of experience, as if some kind of nonhuman thing,
some kind of legendary thing, some kind of impossible
enormity, had been reduced to ordinary human size.
And then it turns out that the poor bastard has bad
teeth, smells funny, and seems to have his whole being
caught up in some kind of insanity, all of his *cells* are
mad, he is composed of a complicated rampage of mad
cells forming one crazy entirety, which is *himself,* virtually unbelievable and altogether unacceptable.

If a boy of ten hadn't ever seen his father, and his
father suddenly showed up, the boy would know some-

thing of what people feel when they meet somebody famous.

So *this* is my father? Well, look at him, for God's sake. He's nothing, he's nobody, he's got hair on his fingers, his nose is out of shape, he smells of tobacco, he seems confused. Is *this* him? Is this actually the man I've heard so much about, thought so much about, the man who is my father and therefore a large part of myself? So *this* is my father. Well, who would ever have thunk it?

Well, in Fresno the king of the Raisin Day Parade one year was Tom Mix. Then, Monte Blue. Then, Bert Lytell. These were the most famous people I saw in the flesh in those days, before I was twelve years of age, and apart from the fact that they rode a chariot and had beside them the Raisin Day Queen, a local girl, elected by members of the social families of the town, Tom Mix, Monte Blue, and Bert Lytell were the same as other men, except for the fact that I had seen them all in silent movies.

Tom Mix was the most impressive, and I wish it had been known in those days that he was a Greek (for that is what I have lately heard). We would all of us had said to one another, "You see Tom Mix up there on that chariot? He's a Greek." Alas, we would have been mistaken. He was not a Greek, after all. Small world, just the same, though.

Bert Lytell on the other hand was only a good actor, in silent films, and then in films *with* sound, and on the stage.

But in films or from the stage of a theater, he didn't have anything like the effect on unfamous people that I have been trying to describe: the strange living reality of the famous person actually alive and standing on two feet.

Meeting certain people makes certain other people literally sick, and that is the sort of thing I am talking about.

Their fame makes people sick, and the reason for this is that their fame or the thing they have that has driven them to fame has made *them* sick. And they have been sick for so long that a stranger feels it immediately upon standing in the presence of that person, and so he also becomes sick.

Try to imagine for instance suddenly meeting Napoleon himself—not one of the many millions of gentle souls who in some strange distortion of meanings have insisted that they are Napoleon. These nice people make you feel sick, too, but perhaps not for the same reason. Although the reasons aren't likely to be much different, at that.

For the original is essentially as mad as the imitator.

That's because each decides to be something he apparently has no real choice about—in short, his decision is helpless, he's caught, he's sick, he's mad.

Or try to imagine meeting Adolph Hitler sometime in 1944, for instance: that would surely have tended to make anybody sick.

And so it might have been to meet Stalin, because

these men were fantastic and preposterous versions of human beings.

Now, sometime before the writing on the wall was clear enough to be readable, namely that a very big war apparently between only Germany and Russia and France was not going to peter out at the Maginot Line but was going to involve the whole world, but especially the United States, I was invited to go to Hyde Park for lunch with Mr. Franklin Delano Roosevelt, along with four or five dozen other writers, actors, and all-around show biz characters, and so I *saw* that fabled gentleman.

Seeing him, however, didn't make me sick, it only made me try to understand why he had to insist on trying to seem to be charming, comic, and adorable, in addition to being great, if that is what he was, or thought he was, or thought he would have to become after the "winning" of the war.

JACK BLACK was a small man who wrote a book about spending half his forty-eight years in American penitentiaries, for robbery. The courts threw the book at him, but he had never done any real first-class robbing, he had done two or three small jobs, without hurting anybody, for enough money to keep him going for perhaps another few days. But he had got caught, and he had begun to do a lot of time, American time, out of the traditional and honorable procedures of American courts, protecting American society.

He finally wrote a letter to Fremont Older, the publisher for William Randolph Hearst of the *San Francisco Call*. Old Fremont Older liked to take up causes and accuse the Judicial and Penological Systems of Corruption and Inhumanity, respectively. Rightfully. He ran front-page stories about how things could go for a hapless man in America—Jack Black, in this instance. He published some of Jack Black's letters in full, and some of his photographs, early and late. And finally Fremont Older sprung Jack Black, with the understanding that, now that he was free, Jack Black would go to work among the poor. He would give talks on the theme that crime doesn't pay.

And of course Jack Black *agreed* to do that, although one can imagine that he would have preferred just to be free.

But when a big newspaper publisher fights the world for you, and sets you free, you are ever after in bondage to him, and to his ideas about what you and your life mean.

I'm glad I met Jack Black, because he was honest, both about himself, his time in penitentiaries, his benefactor, cops, courts, the law, and society.

He said, "A small man becomes a robber more often than an average-sized man, because a small man doesn't like being small," which of course came as a surprise to me, since he himself was a small man, about the size of a boy of twelve, and he was speaking honestly, from personal experience.

And he also said, "Oh, I was guilty, I did the robbing all right, but I was *never* a criminal. And if you want to know the truth, in all the pens I was sent to I saw only half a dozen criminals—the rest are only fools, exactly the same as people on the outside—*exactly,* only they *weren't* on the outside, they were in."

This was interesting, because I had always felt that a man in jail is a man who is not really unlike anybody else. I felt that getting caught and going to jail was a technicality, something that could happen to anybody. All the same, once you have been caught, you are rendered out of the *big* game, and relegated to the *little* game. You are a criminal, if only technically.

I was twenty-two when I met Jack Black, and at that time I was somehow able to believe that people in penitentiaries are not really O.K. They might seem to be, but in a showdown they would not be O.K.

It never seemed to occur to me that that was true of people anywhere. It was Jack Black who brought this truth home to me.

I now consider putting anybody *at all* in jail an indication that the culture involved is underdeveloped —*savages* don't fool with jails. They may kill in war or anger, but they don't rub a man's soul out of him with long dead time away from the company of the rest of the sons of bitches of the world.

I spent only from about half past eleven in the morning to half past three in the afternoon one day with Jack Black: I enjoyed a nice Rotarian Club lunch with him, after which he made his talk, which was really a very sad piece of accommodation to the stuffed shirts in the big dining room.

He was a quiet, dignified little guy, with a soul all shattered. Even so, I was surprised less than a year later when I read in the *Call* that Jack Black had committed suicide by drowning himself in the San Francisco Bay.

31

PAPULIUS WAS the publisher of the *Macaroni Review*.

His office was on the second floor of a rattletrap building on Howard Street, where the winos lived the philosophic life, and still do, between Fourth and Fifth Streets in San Francisco.

Overlooking the street was one large room in which he had a desk with a telephone on it, a few copies of the *Macaroni Review,* and three wire baskets containing a great variety of pieces of paper, letters, pamphlets, clippings, and anything else that had come to him in the mail, or by handout.

At the top of one basket, for instance, was a religious pamphlet entitled, "Do You Want to Live

Forever?" (I gather that he was giving the question his best attention.)

He was a slim keyed-up man with a strong Greek accent. (Many years later when I listened to Spyrous Skouras I immediately remembered Papulius. But then you might well ask, Who is Spyrous Skouras?)

Papulius was about thirty-eight to my twenty-four in 1932. He had put a short ad in the classified section of the *Examiner,* which I examined every morning free of charge in the display frame at the Hearst Building, at Third and Market Streets.

The ad said something along the lines of "Writer wanted. Papulius. 848 Howard." This meant that he had got the ad into the paper at the lowest possible cost, but I couldn't be bothered about a detail like that, the thing that got me was that straight-out statement about what he wanted. Writer.

Well, that was me all right, and it didn't matter that there was no word about wages. Were the wages to be by the hour, by the day, by the week, month, year, or perhaps by the piece? If the writer wrote an especially good piece, would this man, this publisher, Papulius, show his appreciation by paying a little something extra? And in those days a little something extra was highly cherished, for the reason that a little something without anything extra was just about the highest achievement any young man could make.

"Papulius," I thought, as I hurried at half past nine one morning in June to 848 Howard Street. "Where have I heard that name before? Isn't it the

name of one of the greatest and noblest Greek philoso-
phers, and isn't this man at 848 Howard Street a de-
scendant of that great Greek?"

Well, whoever he was I would soon know.

When I climbed the stairs to the second floor I saw
a door marked THE MACARONI REVIEW. I knocked
softly, waited, and then tried the knob. It turned, so I
went in.

A very intense little woman with rather insane
eyes, and taut muscles, glanced in my direction, while
a man who wore a very seedy gray Vandyke beard,
standing across a table from the woman, not in anything like a game of ping-pong or anything like that, but
in some kind of activity involving open books and long
lists, this seedy man not only turned and glanced in my
direction but actually asked, "Papulius?"

"Yes, the ad in the paper."

"Well," the man said, "he'll be in in about an hour,
I suppose. Come back in an hour."

"Is the job open?"

"Oh, yes, yes, yes," the man said. "The job is
open."

"The ad said writer wanted."

"Yes, yes, that's right, talk to Mr. Papulius about
it."

An hour later when I went back Papulius received
me with enormous cordiality, and said I was just in time
to go along with him on some calls. He drove to a
spaghetti factory in the North Beach, and, talking
quickly, extracted not one hundred dollars, not fifty

dollars, not forty dollars but *thirty* dollars in cash money from a spaghetti manufacturer for a full-page ad in the next issue of the *Macaroni Review*.

Papulius wanted me to learn to call on such people and to get them to advertise in the magazine, six copies of which he showed me in the car.

The magazine consisted of about forty rather thick slick pages in which there were many full-page advertisements from spaghetti manufacturers.

"There are eighty-four spaghetti and macaroni manufacturers in San Francisco alone," Papulius said with a certain amount of astonishment and pleasure, "and they do not have any other magazine in which to brag, only the *Macaroni Review*. The minute I go to a new customer and open my magazine his eyes pop open, and of course you heard what I told him."

"Yes, you said you would write about his company."

"Exactly," Papulius said. "And you're the writer. On this piece of paper I jotted down his name, and a few facts. Give him a write-up, about a hundred words is enough. Just say he's got a nice clean factory on Columbus Avenue, number 142, he's been making macaroni at this location for eight years, and the family has been in the macaroni business eight generations, something like that."

"Yes, sir," I said, because he hadn't yet come to the money part, the wages, and I figured if I sounded eager and sensible he would mention wages of a certain dignity, but he didn't mention wages of any kind at all, so that I was ready to consider rather undignified wages, even.

We went four blocks in his old Overland to another prospect, and he made the same pitch, but this time the macaroni maker said, "I no need advertise, I got too much business already."

"Prestige! Prestige!" Papulius shouted, *"That's* the reason we want to advertise."

But the macaroni maker waved his arms and said, "I no want what you say," and walked away.

Papulius said, "I did it wrong, it was my fault, learn from my mistakes, I should have mentioned his mother, remember that, with certain big men speak softly of their mothers and they begin to listen, that man didn't listen."

After stopping at half a dozen more places, and after he had won two more advertisers, we went back to his office, and he quicky made a phone call.

"Hello, is that you, dentist? I got some people coming from Sacramento for dinner, I want the teeth cleaned—right away. No time to lose. I be over in five minutes."

And he hung up.

"Have you met Mr. and Mrs. Goostenhouse?" Papulius said, and I thought, "Not officially, and let's just keep it that way, too." But Papulius hollered out, "Come in here, you two."

After they arrived, almost running, he said, "I want you to meet my writer, this boy has got it. He's going to do the writing and the hustling both. Tell Mr.

and Mrs. Goostenhouse your name."

I said my name quickly, and the little tense husband and the little insane wife nodded, and Papulius shouted, "All right, back to your work." And sure enough they went trotting back to their tiny space in the outer office.

"What do they do?" I said.

"They do *something*," Papulius said. "I don't know. I give them the space, free rent, they answer the door and the phone when I'm out. They fool around with dogs, I think. They look like dogs, too. All right, this office is also your office, this desk is also your desk, that typewriter over there, that's also your typewriter, write something for the *Review,* I'll read it tomorrow."

And he went out, to get his teeth cleaned for dinner.

After he was gone Mr. Goostenhouse and his wife stayed away for about an hour, during which time I wrote what I thought was a literary essay about eating, about wheat, flour, water, salt, the discovery of new usages for flour, the meaning of Italy, and the marvel of macaroni—all in well under a thousand words.

I was revising the essay when the husband and wife came into the office and picked up pieces of paper from the wire baskets, and then stopped to chat.

They were breeders of dogs—but only of the very rarest of breeds, not popular dogs.

They showed snapshots of three of these breeds and the dogs looked strangely not unlike the husband and wife.

"May we read what you've written?" the man said, and standing together they read it.

"You *are* a writer," the man said. "But this isn't what he wants."

The following day, after reading the piece, Papulius said, "This is great—we feature it. We go hustle now."

Three days later I stopped going up there, that's all, because he didn't pay wages, and I didn't even want to *try* to earn a living from wheedling money for macaroni ads from sensible men who just couldn't quite resist the fame of having a full-page ad in a fine magazine, and for only $22.50.

32

PAPULIUS WASN'T the only one of his kind. There were others like him, and the thing they shared was a confidence that at a time of national depression they could still beat the system, and make a go of something that didn't really have a chance.

They were loners of one kind or another, even when they were attached to a big outfit and had to do their work according to the rules of policy. Even when they received written instructions about how to perform their work, they chose to follow another course.

Wolinsky at Postal Telegraph in Fresno, in 1922, was theoretically only a roving troubleshooter, working out of Denver and covering the whole Pacific Coast, with instructions coming daily by telegraph both from Denver and from New York.

He was thirty-four to my fourteen, and we were almost the same height, about five feet seven or eight, although I was all muscle and bone, and he was all blubber and smiles.

He liked nothing better than to work hard, and at the same time to hear a joke and to laugh, or to tell a joke and to hear somebody else laugh.

He was the fastest telegrapher in the world, according to the other telegraphers of Fresno, and he had the amazing ability to send a very important telegram full of hard words and numbers by Morse code and at the same time to carry on a loud lively conversation.

He had a kind of double-mind, and a double-concentration system.

Even though he was an outsider, sent in to survey the overall situation in Fresno, and should on this account alone be resented, he was liked by everybody, from the manager, J. D. Tomlinson, to the newest messenger—myself.

He worked as a telegrapher, sending or receiving, only when telegrams had piled up and he didn't want the pride of the company to be belittled—the important thing was the speed with which telegrams were picked up by messengers, the speed with which they were dispatched by telegraphers, and then the speed with which they were delivered, from Fresno to New York, for instance, sometimes in a matter of under twenty minutes.

In those days long distance phone calls were not common. They were far more expensive than sending a telegram, and sometimes the connections were very bad.

Wolinsky's real work was to study the region and to extract the truth about it, with emphasis on the amount of the real and potential telegraph business, who was presently getting most of it, and who was *going* to get a lot more of it, very suddenly.

Well, in Fresno, the real telegraph business was related to the grape and raisin growing, packing, and shipping business, and Western Union was getting most of it.

Whenever anybody sent a telegram by Postal Telegraph, at the very same rates, it was because he had found out that Postal Telegraph had absolutely nothing to do with the United States Post Office, that it was a private company, and that the only competetive, or extra, thing it had to offer was greater speed and accuracy than Western Union.

And it was Wolinsky's job to spread this information among the people who sent telegrams, and to train others to spread it.

He taught me, for instance.

"Always let somebody who sends a telegram know you will get it to its destination immediately—if not sooner." After waiting for me to laugh, he would go on. "Tell them, and then tell them again, Postal is a telegraph company, it is *not* part of the Post Office. Our rates are exactly the same as the rates at Western Union, but our service is *better*—swifter and more accurate. And then, *prove* it."

Now and then there would be an excellent opportunity to demonstrate the superior ability of Postal Telegraph in competition with Western Union.

D. H. Bagdasarian, for instance, sent two telegrams to the same person in Boston, one by Postal, the other by Western Union. The test was the idea of Wolinsky, who sat in Bagdasarian's packinghouse office on Tulare Street at First Avenue. The messenger from Postal Telegraph arrived to pick up the telegram in eight minutes, the messenger from Western Union arrived in twelve. The reply arrived by Postal in forty-eight minutes, and by Western Union in just under two hours.

"All right," D. H. Bagdasarian said. "I go with you, Mr. Wolinsky."

What was Wolinsky's first name? Whatever it was, he was the man who got fat, as I wrote in one of my stories long, long ago, after he died of it.

WHEN I FIRST began to make the scene in Paris from the fifth-floor flat at 74 Rue Taitbout the year was 1960, and I was a mere fifty-two years of age. There was no reason for me not to take the five flights of stairs fairly quickly, and so I did, and it did me more good than harm, as far as I know.

When I got up in the morning I went down for a copy of the *Paris Herald,* as it was called at that time, and a crusty loaf of Paris bread in one or another of its various sizes, the most popular of which was (and is) the *bagguette,* as it is called. A larger, longer, and broader loaf goes under the name of *Parisienne,* and a smaller loaf is called *ficelle.*

I'd pick up one or another of these crusty loaves, hot from the oven, one might say, generally the *bag-*

guette, and I would bound back up to the flat. The water in the kettle would soon be boiling, I'd make a pot of tea, and I would sit down at the card table, the very same red-top card table at which I am now seated, at this typewriter, and I would have tea and fresh bread and Greek cheese and black olives, and then I would clear away the eating stuff and go to work at writing.

I always believe that whenever I am in Paris my first job is to write.

It is not to get married. It is not to find a rich and attractive woman, a riot in bed, and marry her. It is not to fetch all manner of young girls and mature women to bed, although now and then I would invite somebody up, for its own sake, no strings attached, no questions asked, no demands made. I mention this because whenever anybody thinks of Paris, especially whenever Americans think of Paris, they think of the Folies Bergère and juicy Algerian ladies bumping bumps like no American ever learned how, and ooh la la, girls girls girls, as some of the songs of the turn of the century used to put it.

Everybody thinks Paris is one big roaring lark, and it isn't, no city is, that's all part of the tourist racket.

My job in Paris from the beginning has been to do my work, because when a man reaches fifty he knows he isn't forty, and he certainly isn't thirty, but he is still himself, and he still has his work, so is he going to do his work, or is he going to quit?

Well, I didn't give the matter any thought at all, certainly not of that kind, I simply wanted to work, and there was a good reason why. I needed the money.

I had to have money, and I couldn't get any by any other means. My work was writing, so after the sensible breakfast of tea and bread and cheese every morning I went straight to work, and after I had done what I considered a fair day's work I took to the stairway again and went out to walk in the neighborhood.

This is something all writers will understand.

It is so good to have the day's work done that just to be out in the street, free, and to be walking, is a great joy.

I look into windows, especially into the windows of bookstores, which in Paris also sell maps and gifts and all sorts of other things, and are not strictly speaking bookstores at all. But the secondhand book stores, they *are* really book stores, and so I soon knew where they were and I went to them every day.

One of the best was at the end of Lamartine, just across Poissonière, where Lamartine becomes Montholon. This store had a good assortment of old books in English, and I enjoyed browsing through them, and choosing two or three at one franc each, or about twenty cents each, although some of the very best books were only fifty centimes each, or a dime.

The owner himself was about seventy-four years of age, and for three years we were courteous friends, although we never exchanged any words excepting routine French ones.

Then, one day he came to me and said in the

Armenian language, "I have been told you are Saroyan, is that true?"

We became *new* friends, but by doing so we lost something that I am not sure wasn't better.

34

THE WAY to remember people is systematically by time and place, but that's only done, or attempted, when the one who is remembering is doing it for a purpose, for the record, for the archives even, or for his memoirs, or for his autobiography, or for a history of the world he knew, or a history of the human race he met and experienced, and he wants everything to be in the kind of sensible order that does not exist in nature, is not permitted to exist in nature.

Human memory works its own wheel, and stops where it will, entirely without reference to the last stop, and with no connection with the next.

This morning a man remembers riding a wagon somewhere vague and hearing the man holding the reins make a sound to the horse, and tonight this same man remembers seeing a stranger a week ago in the street, whom he instantly believed he had seen in precisely the same manner, somewhere in a street, twenty or thirty years ago, and even then, as now, he had thought the words "my father," and hadn't paid much attention to the man the first time or the second time, or to his having thought the same words both times, or without thinking about his father for longer than *that* instant, and going on to other thoughts and memories and dreams of words, meanings, and mysteries.

The world to every new arrival is an instantaneous grab-bag of known and unknown people, ideas, declarations, secrets, purposes, menaces, joys, comedians, sorrows, jokes, songs, sounds, and punctuation marks from such creatures as birds, who come and go freely to trees, fences, and porch railings. Messages from such animals as rabbits, squirrels, gophers, all with fascinating ways of being, and incredible eyes. Free animals, not like cats and dogs captured in the house and family, or like cows and horses, goats and sheep, unknowingly living to serve and feed human beings.

In the midst of all this, there he is suddenly, *himself,* beginning to become acquainted with the truth of that strange reality. Himself. That which he has once seen, he begins to notice that he can see again, for having seen it *at all,* the first time. Seen then, and now, because it is there now, and was there then, in itself, and in him, and he remembers it, sometimes on purpose, sometimes helplessly.

And so, theoretically, any writer who is concerned

about a chronicle of people he has met is expected to refer to them chronologically. In the case of certain loud eccentrics in the world of art and expression, a beginning is made at the very beginning, and a famous painter, for instance, says he remembers suddenly becoming himself when his father's sperm met his mother's ovum, and wham, as he put it, there he was, wild in the eye, and forever after looking. Looking at everybody and everything, and then painting it the way he saw it, which is the truthful way, he said, not the way it *seems* to be at all. All things are distorted, he said, everything is a part of a huge distortion, the whole universe is a distortion, a tearing to pieces of things that were perhaps once whole, and an exploding of these terrible pieces, and a terrible drowning of them in terrible oceans a billion times larger than Lake Wahtoke in 1919, near Fresno.

And then this terrible eccentric—myself of course, just invented—goes on to say that memory follows no rules, and thus, the owner of the bookshop on Montholon, whom I took to be a Frenchman, who turned out to be an Armenian, began to *fade* as the smiling gentleman at his desk accepting small coins for old books, a *real* friend, somebody memory would hang onto for a long time. And soon after the revelation, talking in Armenian each time we met, the quiet man seemed to be forgotten, seemed even never to have existed, and of course it is the quiet man who is memorable, and the other who is only another talking compatriot, proud and respectful.

Thus, Girard became Jirayr, and the real language of human beings, unspoken, became Armenian, spoken.

35

THE VERY FIRST time I reached Paris, in April or
May of the year of 1935, I had been met at Gare St.-
Lazare by a short excited Frenchman who looked more
as if he might be English or German, for he was thick
and intensely earnest, as if he were engaged in very
important business, possibly spying or secret service,
and he wore a black derby.

I used to be able to know from a fair distance if
somebody was concerned about meeting *me,* and this
happened when I saw this man, who had a piece of
paper in his hand. I didn't know that I was to be met
at the railway station at all, although at Southampton
somebody from a travel agency had rounded up six or
seven of us and had put us into one compartment of the
train to London, where we were again met by another

travel man who put us into a bus which took us to an unnamed small hotel where bed and breakfast cost about the equivalent of a dollar and a half.

Those were the days, one might say. I certainly felt as if I were a rich millionaire, as the joke goes.

Now, at the Paris railway station, here was this man, looking for somebody.

I walked straight up to him, and he said, "Saroyan?"

He pronounced the name in the European manner, which is the proper way to pronounce it.

He then said, "Welcome to Paris. I have an excellent room waiting for you, at the Atlantic Hotel on Rue Londres, shall we walk?"

I had only one suitcase, which he felt obliged to seize, and so we went out and walked to the hotel. It never occurred to me that this walk meant a little profit to him, a profit of perhaps as much as half a dollar, for he had been provided with taxi money.

He got me into the hotel, I liked the room, he told me about my next train connection, the following morning at a convenient hour, to Vienna, where I would be met again and escorted to a hotel.

"I shall come here an hour before train time tomorrow," he said, and bowed, removing his derby as he did so, and I thought, "Boy, it's good to be famous. This is just like in a movie. Here I am a world traveler, honored on all sides by people who smile at me and look at my picture in my passport, and then at me, and write my name very carefully in the register, and they know, they suspect, that this is not just a common name, this name is a famous name, it belongs to a man of the world, a man of art, a writer, an observer, a thinker, one of the immortals. Me."

And only *half*-kidding. I felt simultaneously elated and very nearly exhausted, for I tend to react intensely to everything and everybody I reach. The result is that days of ocean travel, hours of walks in London, hundreds of people on the Channel boat, on the train, in the station, in the Paris streets, all of these people, all of these scenes come to me with great force and make a powerful impact—something I had never before noticed, although in a lesser degree it had always been going on.

I have many times seen men not unlike the man in the black derby who met me at Gare St.-Lazare, and I have invariably considered each of them a friend, with a little larceny in his nature. Nothing spectacular, just a slightly cut corner, a walk of two blocks with a suitcase, carried by the man himself, in order to save, and thus to have, about half a dollar.

The innocence of these people has always impressed me as being even better if not quite as pure as the innocence of people who have not been tempted.

There was a floating crap game in the summer of 1922 in Fresno, in which the take of the house was dropped into a cigar box by an Armenian boy whose nickname was Turk. During a big game in a big room at the Sequoia Hotel, Turk would remove the take from the various pots, so that soon the cigar box would have a total of at least two hundred dollars in it.

Well, when the game was robbed by four masked bandits, Turk refused to give up the cigar box saying, "You can't take this, this is the take."

That's innocence. But of course the box *was* taken. And Turk felt that he had let himself down by not losing his life in refusing to give up the box.

36

I WORKED on a vineyard with a retired Armenian wrestler named Nazaret Torosian one year, and he is one of the few people I believe I have ever learned a little something or other from, for he frequently stopped in his work to say, "If your opponent gets a headlock on you, feel out the action of his muscles, and when the pattern of tension and relaxation is known, wait for the next instant of relaxation, and then leap upward with all the force you can manage, and I think you will find that you can break free from his hold upon your head."

"Yes, sir," I used to say, "but in leaping up is it not possible that the top of my head will strike the bottom of his head, his *chin,* and be considered a foul?"

"No, sir," the retired wrestler would reply. "In

making your break for freedom, the force of your movement automatically drives him out of the line of your
released head, but let us say that somehow or other his
chin *is* in fact directly in line with your head, and that
the top of your head *does* strike him on the bottom of
his chin—all the better, my boy. Don't worry about it,
you will scarcely feel the impact, whereas he may be
pushed close to unconsciousness by the force under his
chin."

"Yes, sir," I used to say, "I'll remember that."

And so we might not speak again for ten minutes,
or even twenty, and now and then not even for an hour,
because pruning muscat vines calls for a certain amount
of concentration, and at the same time in noticing the
beauty of the structure of the vine one tends to fall
silent.

But sooner or later the Armenian wrestler would
stand up straight and say, "If you are on the mat, and
he's sprawling all over you to keep your back flat on the
mat so that he may win the round, God help you, that's
all I can say."

"Yes, of course," I used to say, "but is there nothing I can do to stop him from keeping my back flat on
the mat?"

"Yes, there is," the old wrestler would say, "but it
isn't easy, it is almost impossible, everything happens
very swiftly in wrestling, and when you are off balance
in that manner, where is your strength to come from?
You are flat, and you have nothing to hold your
strength together *upon,* for a counterattack. But there

is one thing you can do, and again it is something more in the realm of art than athletics, and I myself in a long career of professional wrestling was able to do it only perhaps half a dozen times out of at least a hundred opportunities."

"And what is that?" I would ask.

"Disappear," Nazaret Torosian would say. "And I *mean* just that. Disappear, out from under. How it happens I have never been able to understand, and I have studied the matter from every possible angle. My wrestling weight was 240 pounds, all muscle, bone, and cartilege, and so we know that this is a great deal of body to cause to disappear, and yet, that is precisely what happened at least half a dozen times. I was flat on my back and my opponent—once he was Strangler Lewis himself, another time he was Jimmy Londos, and another time he was Stanislaus Szabisco—and then suddenly I was *not* flat on my back, I was *up,* on my feet, and he was just turning to see where I had gone. So I invariably thought to myself, Now, how did that happen? And of course I went on and won the round. The matches in those days were the best two out of three, as I think you may remember."

"Yes," I would reply. "Yes, sir, I *do* remember, but after you had given the matter a great deal of thought, what did you conclude? How did it happen that you were able to disappear in that manner? What was it that permitted that impossible disappearance?"

"Well," Nazaret said, "I finally decided that it was Christianity. Jesus did it. Our blessed babe worked another miracle. It is not for nothing that we are the first nation in the world to accept Jesus. It was Christianity that did it."

"Yes, sir," I used to say, "but your opponents, they also were Christians, every one of them."

The wrestler would look up and consider what I had said, and then he would say, "What you say is true, but we are Armenian Christians, and that gives us just the edge we need. An Irish Christian, a Greek Christian, a Polish Christian—Jesus *will* help them, but only *after* he has helped an Armenian Christian."

I have never had occasion to use any of the wrestler's advice, however.

Or so I seem to believe, at any rate.

But who says I am a Christian? With me, in religion, it has got to be all or none, and none is just an edge too little and belittling. Chance meetings with living saints and sons of bitches go on and on.